THE SILENT KILLER

When widower Sidney Middleton is found dead from carbon monoxide poisoning, Sheila Malory is deeply disturbed. The old man had seemed in rude health and the official explanation that the ageing wood-burning stove was faulty just doesn't seem to add up. Then there's the fact that his son, David Middleton, had been keen in recent months to pack his father away to a nursing home. Suspecting that this was no accidental death, Sheila uncovers some rather shocking information which paints Sidney in a very different light – how many people might have borne him a grudge?

THE SILENT KILLER

THE SILENT KILLER

by

Hazel Holt

Magna Large Print Books
Long Preston, North Yorkshire,
BD23 4ND, England.

British Library Cataloguing in Publication Data.

Holt, Hazel
   The silent killer.

A catalogue record of this book is
available from the British Library

ISBN   0-7505-2237-2

First published in Great Britain 2004 by Allison & Busby Ltd.

Published in Large Print 2004 by arrangement with
Allison & Busby Ltd.

Magna Large Print is an imprint of Library Magna Books Ltd.

Printed and bound in Great Britain by
T.J. (International) Ltd., Cornwall, PL28 8RW

For James and Hilary Hale, but for whom...

1

'I suppose,' Rosemary said regretfully, 'there's no earthly point in keeping them.' She smoothed down the pile of blankets on the bed. 'I did offer them to Jilly but, of course, they use duvets too.'

'I suppose you could give them to Oxfam,' I suggested. 'They always seem to want blankets for refugees.'

Rosemary looked down doubtfully at the pastel colours and the satin bindings. 'Do you think these are the sort they mean?'

'I should think they'd be jolly glad to get any sort of blanket.'

'Anyway, I don't think Oxfam sends out the actual blankets one donates. I think they're recycled or something and the money is spent on the sort of blankets refugees need.'

'Oh,' I said, rejecting with reluctance the picture of refugees wrapped in pure wool, pale blue blankets edged with satin ribbon. 'Oh well, I suppose it is more practical. Though I would have thought the nice

9

colours might have cheered them up a bit.'

'Well, whatever. They'll have to go. I really must have a proper turn out. I can't think why I keep half the things that are cluttering up the house.'

'Oh I know,' I agreed. 'It's quite impossible. I've got a whole chest full of white damask table linen all wrapped up in black tissue paper. Now what am I going to do with *that?*'

'Actually,' Rosemary said, 'I believe you can sell it. There's a woman at South Molton who sells antique linen.'

'I don't know that you'd call it *antique*,' I said doubtfully.

'Don't you believe it. Anything can be antique nowadays.'

'Most of them,' I said, 'were part of my mother's trousseau. Of course that was in the nineteen twenties, when brides still had trousseaux!'

'There you are then, definitely antiques.'

'I hardly ever used them myself. Just occasionally when we were first married and I had to give dinner parties for Peter's important clients. But the laundry bills were so horrendous and I couldn't possibly wash them myself – all that starching!'

'Can you still get starch, I wonder?'

'Probably not. Nor blue bags or soap or Monkey Brand... Oh dear,' I 'I'm beginning to feel distinctly myself.'

Rosemary laughed. 'Come on, let's go downstairs and I'll put the kettle on.'

'I suppose,' I said when we were comfortably settled at Rosemary's kitchen table with tea and chocolate digestives, 'we are better off now, with all our modern conveniences.'

'When they work,' Rosemary said. 'I had to wait the best part of a week for the man to come and see to the washing machine. By the end of the second day I'd gladly have settled for an old fashioned washtub and a mangle!'

'Still... Oh, by the way, talking of old fashioned things, I'm looking for someone to go and collect some stuff from Sidney Middleton. He's promised us some furniture for the Red Cross auction sale and I can't find anyone with a trailer or van or anything to fetch it in.'

'Somebody else having a clear-out?'

'I believe he's thinking of going into an old people's home – or his son is thinking of it for him. I don't think Sidney's very keen on the idea.'

'He must be quite old. He seems to have

11

ᵥed at Lamb's Cottage forever!'

'In his eighties, I think – though I suppose that's not so old nowadays. Do you know I saw a whole *rack* of ninetieth birthday cards in Passmore's the other day!'

'Yes, he must be eighty-something, because his wife went to school with Mother.'

'Anyway,' I said, 'whatever he gives us will be very good quality – he's really quite well off – and should fetch a decent price.'

'Do you think he will go into a Home?'

'I don't see why he should, he's still quite fit. A bit absent-minded sometimes, but then aren't we all?'

'I *know*,' Rosemary agreed. 'Do you know, the other day I simply *couldn't* think of the name hydrangea, and nor could Jack. It drove us nearly mad. In the end I had to ring up Jilly and ask her. I expect she thinks we're both going senile.' She poured us both another cup of tea and continued, 'And when I go into the larder for something I can't remember what I went in for and have to go back into the kitchen to think what it was.'

'Oh, so do I! And isn't it extraordinary that it always seems to work. I suppose when it doesn't we'll know that we're really going into Alzheimers!'

Rosemary bit thoughtfully into a biscuit. 'No, I think David Middleton is afraid that he and Bridget may have to look after the old man and that wouldn't suit their lifestyle!'

'Oh yes,' I said. 'All that back and forth to their house in Provence and cruises round the Greek islands. No, it certainly wouldn't.'

'No, what they would like is for him to sell Lamb's Cottage – it must be worth a lot with all that land – and have him quietly fade away in a Home. You know the way people do once they've left their own homes, they just seem to give up.'

'It would be so sad. Poor old Sidney – he's such a dear man. Why is it that so many nice people have such horrible relations?'

'I don't think Bridget is so bad,' Rosemary said. 'I feel quite sorry for her sometimes, David is pretty horrid to her as well.'

'Mm,' I agreed, 'she does look a bit downtrodden. Anyway, we'll be very glad of Sidney's things. We haven't got anything substantial so far, just a lot of bits and pieces. So, do you know anyone?'

'Anyone?'

'Who could collect the stuff.'

'Oh no, sorry. I can't think of a soul.'

13

'Oh well, I'll just have to see what Michael can fit in his Land Rover.'

I went with Michael to Lamb's Cottage that weekend and I thought Sidney was looking a bit subdued, not his usual ebullient self.

'Come on in,' he said. 'I've got the kettle on.' He led the way into the house. 'You don't mind sitting in the kitchen, do you? I more or less live in it now, especially in the winter.'

'I'm not surprised,' I said, looking around me appreciatively. 'It's very cosy.'

It was a large farmhouse kitchen with a big wood-burning stove. Heavy dressers filled with china took up most of the wall space and there was a big window, whose broad sill held pots of herbs and flowering plants. As well as a big kitchen table with four upright chairs there were a couple of comfortable armchairs and a television set on one of the dressers.

'Joan loved her kitchen,' Sidney said, 'and when she died I somehow felt more at home here than in the sitting room.'

'It's lovely,' I said, 'and blissfully warm on a cold day like this!'

'Yes, the stove's very good, but it's been playing up a bit lately. I keep meaning to get someone in to have a look at it.'

He poured the tea and pushed a plate of biscuits towards us.

'I've put the things in the hall,' he said. 'A couple of little tables, a chest of drawers, two bookcases and some other odds and ends – well, you'll see for yourself. All the big stuff will have to go to the sale rooms, I suppose. That is if I decide to go.'

'You haven't decided yet, then?' Michael asked.

Sidney shrugged. 'I could hang on here for a bit, I suppose. I'm a bit creaky but there's nothing really wrong with me. Mrs Harrison comes in twice a week to keep the house clean and tidy...' His voice trailed off.

'Well then,' I said, 'why move out?'

'The thing is,' Sidney said earnestly, 'I don't want to be a burden to David. He's still making his way in the world and has quite enough on his mind as it is without having to worry over me.'

Michael and I exchanged glances, since worrying about his father has never seemed to us to be uppermost in David Middleton's mind.

'And actually,' Sidney went on, 'he's found me this very nice retirement home down in Devon. He took me to see it last Sunday. A

15

beautiful big room – en suite of course – and the grounds were magnificent. It's almost on the coast and on a clear day I believe you can see the sea.'

'Devon!' I said. 'That's a long way away! It wouldn't be easy for him to visit you – or all your friends.'

'But you haven't decided anything yet?' Michael asked.

'Well, no, not exactly decided. I told David I'd think about it. But that's why I'm getting rid of some things – just to show willing, as it were.'

'Well,' I said bluntly, 'I think you should stay where you are. You're managing perfectly well and,' I added, 'no trouble to anyone! Besides, I'm sure Lamb's Cottage holds so many happy memories for you.'

His face lit up. 'Oh yes. Joan loved it here. We bought it before I retired, you know – used to come down for every holiday and weekends, too, when we could manage it. The day we moved back here from London was the happiest day of our lives!'

'There you are then!'

'But David...'

'You're not going to be a burden to anyone for years yet!' I said. 'You stay where you are.'

'But I don't suppose he will,' I said to Michael as we drove back home. 'David Middleton will keep on at him until he gets what he wants. Horrid man!'

'I'm afraid you're right. Poor old thing, he's too nice for his own good.' He sounded his horn at a pheasant who was contemplating a suicidal dash across the road. 'Oh, by the way, Thea said could you possibly look after your granddaughter on Thursday afternoon? She's got to do a few things in Taunton and doesn't want to take Alice with her. She could drop her off with you on the way.'

It was while I was taking Alice along the sea-front in her pushchair (she was teething and not her usual placid self) that I met Bridget Middleton walking her spaniel.

'Hello, Bridget – look, Alice, at the nice doggie. How are you?'

'Oh, hello, Sheila. Not bad. Busy, you know.'

'Yes, I know.'

Though I couldn't imagine what Bridget could be busy with. She was at home all day ('David doesn't want me to have a job') and her two boys were away at boarding school. She did a certain amount of charity work ('David says it's important to put something back into the community') and I suppose she did some entertaining in their big house just outside Taviscombe – but still...

'Oh, is this your granddaughter?' Bridget leaned over the pushchair and peered in at Alice, who had just fallen asleep. 'Isn't she a pet!'

'Mercifully asleep now,' I said. 'She's a bit fractious at the moment – teething.'

'Poor little mite! But I love them at that age, they're so sweet and loving. And a girl too – I always wanted a girl.'

'You must miss the boys,' I said, 'away at school.'

'Yes,' she said wistfully, 'I do.'

'My brother was at boarding school,' I told her. 'It was the usual thing then, but I didn't want Michael to go away. After all, there are some very good schools quite near where they can be day-boys.'

'Oh, I know! And I do so wish... But David said that it was important for them to go to a top public school – useful contacts, you know.'

'Yes, I see.' I rocked the pushchair gently to and fro. 'Michael and I went to Lamb's Cottage last weekend. Sidney is very kindly giving us some things for the Red Cross auction.'

'Oh, really.'

'We thought he was looking very well.'

'Oh... David says he's getting very frail.'

'Well,' I said firmly, 'we didn't see any sign of that. In fact we both thought how well he's coping.'

'He's quite old, though.'

'The eighties aren't that old nowadays,' I said briskly. 'Lots of people stay in their own homes well into their nineties and still look after themselves perfectly well. Besides, Sidney has help in the house and the garden.'

'But it's such a responsibility,' Bridget said earnestly. 'Say he had a stroke or something and lay there for days and nobody knew!'

'Mrs Harrison would. And I'm sure she'd look in every day if you're really worried. Besides, there are those splendid things you can wear round your neck to call for help.'

'I suppose so...' she said doubtfully.

'And there's all sorts of help you can get from the Social Services to stay in your own home.'

'Oh, I don't think David would like *that!*' Bridget said quickly. 'Anyway, they're for poor people, aren't they?'

'I'm sure they'd let you pay,' I said. 'If you insisted.'

Bridget looked at me, suspicious of an irony she had not quite understood. 'Anyway,' she said, 'David's found this marvellous place in Devon for him. More like a hotel than an Old People's Home. It's very expensive. I'm sure his father would love it, and there'd be lots of company for him. He'd like that.'

The spaniel, as if sensing her uneasy mood, began to whimper and pull at his lead.

'Oh dear,' she said gratefully, 'Dandy's getting restless, I must go. Lovely to have seen you.'

'She's obviously got a guilty conscience about it,' I said to Thea, when she called to collect Alice. 'She's a nice person really I'm sure, and she can't be happy to see the way David is determined to get poor old Sidney out of Lamb's Cottage.'

'Well, Sidney must just stand up to him.'

'Ye-es. But it's not easy when you're old. It would be different if there were two of them. Not,' I added thoughtfully, 'that Joan would have been much good at standing up to anyone.'

'Really? I don't actually remember her and she'd died before I came back to Taviscombe.'

'Yes, I suppose she had, it was quite a while ago – goodness, how the time flies! No, Joan was a sweet person, but a mouse-like little creature who couldn't say boo to a goose.'

'Do mice speak to geese?' Thea asked, laughing.

'No, you know what I mean. Quiet and gentle, a real homebody, as they say I often wondered how she managed when they were in London – he was a very high-powered accountant – and there must have been a lot of entertaining. And he was away quite a bit because his firm had connections in America, so she was on her own because David was away at boarding school. As far as I can gather she never really had friends of her own and her brother lived in Canada – she must have been lonely. Of course she was absolutely devoted to Sidney and he was to her. He once told me they were childhood sweethearts and they married very young. They did have their Ruby Wedding before she died.'

'That was nice.'

'It was a terrific do, at that big Country House Hotel just outside Taunton. Michael and I went. I remember thinking at the time that Joan was a bit overwhelmed by it all.

Sidney was in his element, of course, but Joan just sat there looking bewildered.'

Alice, who'd been still asleep (I'd lifted her from her pushchair onto the sofa) showed signs of waking up and started to grizzle a little.

'Poor love,' I said. 'That tooth is still hurting her. Do you think she ought to have some more Calpol?'

'No, she'll be all right. I'll wait until I get her home.'

Alice, now fully awake, caught sight of the various bags and parcels Thea had brought with her and rolled herself off the sofa and trotted over to investigate them. She opened one of the bags, took out a rag doll with fair plaits, dressed in pink gingham, seized it and clambered back onto the sofa again, rocking it in her arms.

'Dolly,' she said triumphantly. 'Alice's dolly.'

'I know,' Thea said defensively, 'she's got so many dolls already, but I had to bring her back something!'

'Better than Calpol,' I said. 'Or any medicine. What else did you get?'

'Oh I must show you. I went mad in Laura Ashley and got her the most gorgeous velvet pinafore dress with an embroidered yoke.

Look! And a dear little hat to go with it.'

When they'd gone I thought again about Bridget and how, in a strange way, she was a sort of replica of Joan, another doormat – so unexpected in this day and age. Thea was modern, in that she'd had a very successful career, but old fashioned because she'd chosen to give up her job to look after Alice. I wondered how it would be with Alice – home or career? Of course I might not still be around to see and the thought saddened me. I poured myself a gin and tonic, partly to cheer myself up and partly because I was out of practice at looking after small children and suddenly felt very tired.

2

It is a truth universally acknowledged (at least among those engaged in Good Works) that committee meetings are (generally speaking) a complete waste of time. A great deal is said but very little is decided and, in the end, the actual work is done by the faithful few who have been doing it for as long as anyone can remember, while those who were most voluble usually find they have important engagements that can't be broken when any sort of action is called for.

'It's ridiculous,' Anthea said as the two of us were toiling away in Brunswick Lodge, the centre of all such activities, sorting out the things donated for the Red Cross auction. 'It's just like last year. And the year before. Maurice Freebody promised *faithfully* to come and help – *and* Norman Hastings. And who has to do it in the end – we do! Men!'

'It's not just those two,' I said crossly. 'Sandra Lewis said leave it all to her and Robert, they'd see to it this year. And then

24

they went off to Malta. Why do people promise these things? They must have had the holiday booked when she said it!'

'Oh, Sandra Lewis!' Anthea exclaimed scornfully. 'She's completely unreliable. She offered to make the mince pies for last year's Christmas concert and two days beforehand – two *days*, mind you! – she rang me up to say that they were having to go up to Nottingham to spend Christmas with Robert's mother!'

'Typical!' I dragged a large wooden box full of assorted china out of the way so that I could get at a pile of old records. 'Some of these things are jolly heavy. All those big pieces of furniture have got to be taken upstairs and there's no way we can do that.'

'What we need,' Anthea said, conveniently forgetting her earlier condemnation of the sex, 'is a man.'

'Exactly. But who? Most of our so-called helpers are either not available or too old. We need new blood. Surely there must be someone who's just retired – you know, fit and with lots of time.'

Anthea considered this. 'Well, there's the Nortons,' she said. 'They've just moved down here. From Reading, I think. They came to the Wednesday coffee morning last week. He looked quite strong.'

I met them the following Wednesday. Anthea called me over.

'Sheila, do come and meet Myra and Jim Norton.'

'Lovely to meet you, Mrs Malory – or can I call you Sheila? Everyone seems to use Christian names now, I suppose it's friendlier. Anthea's told me so much about you.'

Myra Norton was short and plump and, obviously, very voluble. Jim Norton was tall and, I imagine by necessity, fairly silent. He did, however, look suitably strong for the activities Anthea had in mind.

'How are you?' I said shaking hands. 'Have you been in Taviscombe long?'

'No, only a couple of months. It took us all that time to get settled. Well, you know what it's like, moving. You can never find anything and then one of the boxes went missing. It had all my tablecloths and dusters in it – you can imagine how inconvenient *that* was. I had a terrible time getting it back from the removers. And then, of course, the bungalow here is quite a bit smaller than our house, so it was really quite difficult to fit everything in, though I must say this place has a lovely lot of cupboards.'

'That's nice.'

'The garden's bigger though. I tell Jim there's quite a lot to keep him busy.'

'Not too busy, I hope,' Anthea broke in 'to lend a hand here at Brunswick Lodge.'

'Oh yes,' Myra Norton said eagerly. 'We're looking forward to joining in things, aren't we, Jim?'

Her husband gave a wintry smile but didn't commit himself. Obviously his consent was not considered necessary.

'It's the Red Cross auction,' Anthea said. 'Just a question of another pair of hands to sort things out. Some of the stuff is quite heavy, furniture and so forth.'

'Well,' Myra Norton said, 'isn't that a coincidence? I was saying to Jim only yesterday that we have a few things we really don't have room for. There's that corner cupboard, Jim, you know the one I mean, and the small chest of drawers that used to be on the landing – though, of course we don't have a landing now, living in a bungalow!' She laughed heartily. 'Yes, we'd be really pleased to donate those. I mean, if you put things in the sale rooms you never get anything for them, do you? So I'd much rather they went to a good cause.'

'That's very generous of you,' I said.

'And of course,' Anthea broke in, 'if you,'

she turned to Jim Norton, '*could* very kindly give us a hand with some of the heavy stuff, we'd be most grateful.'

'Well,' Anthea said with satisfaction as we were washing up after the coffee morning, 'I think they'll be quite useful. *She* goes on a bit, but they both seem very willing to help.'

'I don't think he's got much choice in the matter,' I said, laughing.

'Oh well,' Anthea said dismissively, 'as long as he moves that furniture, what does it matter!'

The Red Cross auction was very well attended. It's always popular, partly because of the bargains to be picked up, partly because it's become a social occasion, and partly because Tommy Hunter conducts the proceedings. Tommy, an auctioneer by trade, is a large, genial man with a fund of well-worn witticisms, and immensely popular in the district. To see Tommy in full flow at a cattle auction (his favourite venue) is to see a true professional at work. He'd got the proceedings well under way (the audience nicely warmed up with a selection of the terrible jokes that are his trade-mark) when I saw Sidney Middleton come in. I edged my way round to the back of the room to where he was standing.

'Hello, Sidney, how splendid to see you.'

He smiled. 'I thought I'd just come along to see how it was going,' he said. 'Dick and Marjorie Croft from the village were coming so they gave me a lift.'

'I'm afraid your things have gone already,' I said. 'They all fetched really good prices.'

'That's good.'

'Have you decided yet what you want to do?' I asked.

'No, not really. David's very anxious that I should move before winter sets in.'

'Oh, but Lamb's Cottage is very cosy.'

'It is a bit isolated, I suppose, if the weather's bad.'

'We haven't had a really bad winter for ages,' I said. 'All this global warming!'

Sidney laughed. 'Well, I'll have to see. Good gracious, whatever is that?'

Tommy Hunter was holding up a peculiar object made out of wrought iron. Its shape was amorphous and its purpose enigmatic. Even Tommy appeared to be baffled by it.

'Now who'll make me an offer for this excellent – whatever it is! One thing you can be sure of. If you buy this, you'll be buying something really unique. Now who'll start me off at ten pounds? All right, five pounds.

Come along ladies and gentlemen – look at what you'll be getting for your money. There can't be another of these in the whole of West Somerset! Put it in your garden, frighten the birds away! That lady at the front! Five pounds? Right now, any advance on five pounds? You're missing the bargain of a lifetime! No? All right then. *Sold* to the lady with excellent taste!'

'Who on earth bought that?' Sidney said.

I craned forward. 'Goodness,' I said, 'it's Mrs Norton.'

'Norton?'

'Yes, Myra Norton. She and her husband Jim Norton have just moved down here.'

Myra Norton, catching sight of me, waved enthusiastically – almost inadvertently bidding for a large copper coal scuttle. I waved back, more circumspectly.

'That's her,' I said to Sidney, 'and that's her husband, the tall, melancholy man standing behind her.'

Certainly Jim Norton was looking particularly glum today – though I suppose in view of his wife's recent purchase that wasn't surprising. He leaned forward and spoke to his wife and then turned away from the bidding abruptly and walked out of the room.

30

'Poor man,' I said, 'he probably can't bear to see what she is going to bid for next!'

Sidney laughed. 'It's extraordinary what people will buy on occasions like this. They seem to lose all sense of reason!'

'Thank goodness,' I said. 'It's all for a very good cause.'

'It's been really successful,' Anthea said the next day when we were clearing up. 'Trevor said we cleared nearly three thousand pounds.'

'That's more than last year, isn't it? And not too much stuff left over.'

'A few of the old faithfuls,' Anthea said, holding up a pair of stag's horns mounted on a wooden shield. 'I think these will have to go to the tip this time – no one will buy them now – politically incorrect.'

'I suppose so. Still, you never know. It seems a shame...'

'Well, certainly that chair will have to go, it's got woodworm and is really unsafe, and that box of ornaments and that ghastly firescreen.'

'I'll see if Michael can spare the time,' I said. 'Perhaps tomorrow.'

'No, it's all right, there's no need to bother Michael again. Jim Norton has a trailer and he'll take all the junk things to the tip for us. He said he'd call in today and see what there was and whether he'd have to make several journeys.'

'How splendid! Did he actually offer or did his wife offer for him?'

'No, he came up to me after the sale and was quite chatty.'

'Really?'

'Yes, I was surprised. I think he wants to be involved in things as well as her. He was asking about the various people there and that sort of thing. I was quite pleased, he's just the sort of person we need. *And*,' she added, 'he knows all about electricity so perhaps we can get another point put in the kitchen, you know how inconvenient it is only to have the one.'

'He sounds too good to be true!'

We were just on the point of packing up when Jim Norton appeared.

'Sorry I'm a bit late,' he said, 'but Myra wanted me to help her move some things out of the shed.'

'Oh, that's all right,' Anthea said. 'We've only just finished. Now then, these are the things to go. Do you think you can manage them?'

He surveyed the various items scattered

around and said, 'I think they'll all go in one load.'

'Oh, that would be splendid,' I said. 'Can we give you a hand with moving them?'

'No, no, I can manage.'

'So,' I asked, 'what did you think of the auction?'

'It was very well attended.'

'Practically everything went,' I said, 'even the more peculiar items. Sidney – that's Sidney Middleton – was only saying how extraordinary it is how people will bid for anything!'

'Oh, was Sidney there?' Anthea said. 'I didn't see him.'

'He only popped in for a little while. Dick and Marjory brought him.'

'Well, he was certainly right. That wrought iron thing your wife bought,' Anthea said with her usual lack of tact, 'whatever *was* it?'

'Myra thinks it's a jardiniere. She's going to stand plants on it on the patio.'

'How clever of her to spot it,' I said hastily. 'She must have a good eye for a bargain.'

Jim Norton looked unconvinced.

'Well,' Anthea said, 'if you're sure we can't do anything to help we'll be off. Just slam the front door behind you when you go. It's a Yale lock.'

'And thank you very much for all your help,' I said, anxious to keep this paragon. 'It really is appreciated!'

He mumbled something about it being nothing and began gathering the various objects together in a workmanlike way.

'Well,' I said to Anthea as we were walking along the Avenue together, 'he does seem to be a find! Let's hope we can keep him.'

Things seemed a bit flat after the auction, but as Rosemary said, the next Bring and Buy sale would be on us before we knew where we were and we deserved a little break.

'So,' she said, 'let's go to Taunton next week and have a look at the sales. It shouldn't be too crowded now that the schools have gone back.'

'Oh yes, that would be nice. I'd like to get a few things for Alice – she grows so fast, and some of the children's dresses are so pretty now.'

'Which is more than can be said for the grown up ones,' Rosemary said. 'Quite hideous!'

We spent a happy morning walking through the department stores making disparaging remarks about some of the items on display.

'Honestly,' Rosemary said, stopping in

front of a shapeless garment in violent tangerine, 'how could they imagine *anyone* would buy that, even in the sales?'

'This is worse,' I said, taking a dress from the rack. 'Lime green and purple zigzags – and look at the skirt!'

'Ghastly!'

'I mean,' I went on, 'I know they're meant for the young, but *we* wouldn't have worn these things, would we, even in our giddy youth?'

'Certainly not. In our day, thank goodness, there were dresses that actually made you look more attractive, not less!'

'Come on,' I said, 'let's go up to the children's department and find something pink and frilly.'

Laden with parcels (in spite of any good resolutions I may make beforehand, I always get carried away in the sales) we collapsed into chairs in the café grateful for pots of tea and prawn sandwiches.

'I'm not sure about that top I got for Delia,' Rosemary said, rummaging in the bag to refresh her memory of it. 'I *think* they're still wearing them with those glittery bits. But she's practically a teenager now and she has to wear whatever her friends are wearing.'

'Oh, I think it'll be all right,' I said reassuringly. 'I'm sure I saw one like that in the trailer on television for some sort of pop show.'

'Oh well, we must hope for the best. You make the most of Alice while she's small and doesn't have an opinion on such things – it doesn't last long!'

Rosemary poured herself a second cup of tea.

'It was nice to see Sidney at the auction,' she said. 'I thought he looked very well. Surely there's no need for him to go into a home, is there?'

'No, of course there isn't. It's only the wretched David pushing him. Still, Sidney said he hadn't decided yet, so perhaps he'll stand up to David and stay where he is.'

'It is a problem, though,' Rosemary said thoughtfully. 'I suppose the time will come when we'll have to do something about Mother.'

'Surely not!'

Rosemary's mother, Mrs Dudley, has always seemed to me indestructible, immortal even.

'Oh, she's all right for the moment – she's quite well and pretty mobile, and as long as she has Elsie she'll be fine. But Elsie's in her seventies now and won't go on for ever, even if Mother does!'

'I can't imagine your mother anywhere except in her own home.'

'She'd fight any sort of move every step of the way,' Rosemary sighed. 'I can see battles ahead. I know she's spent the odd week in West Lodge – mainly to keep up with the gossip there! – but I don't think she's ever seriously considered going in there permanently.'

'Oh dear. I didn't have that problem with my mother, of course. I mean, she was an invalid for so long but able to stay at home with us. It was only at the end that she had to go into a nursing home.'

'There's no way we could have Mother to live with us,' Rosemary said. 'Jack would divorce me!'

'Good heavens, no!' I said, shuddering at the thought of the battle of wills between those two strong-minded people. 'It doesn't bear thinking about!'

Rosemary picked up a stray prawn from her plate and ate it.

'Getting old,' I said, 'I mean *really* old, is horrible. Do you think we'll be as difficult to our children?'

'Certainly not,' Rosemary said briskly, 'we

have much sweeter natures. No, we'll be like poor Sidney, not wanting to be a nuisance, taking ourselves off to a retirement home at the first hint of feebleness.'

'What a dismal thought,' I said. 'Oh well, with that in view I'm going to have a slice of that delicious looking chocolate cake while I still can. How about you?'

3

'What on earth are you cooking?' Michael asked as he came into the kitchen.

'It's only Foss's fish,' I said, taking it out of the microwave. 'Be an angel and open the window to let the smell out, will you?'

'It's a bit stiff,' he said, wrestling with the catch. The window flew open with a jerk and he examined the frame. 'You really need to do something about these windows. Look, the sill outside is quite rotten.'

'I know,' I sighed, 'but it's so difficult to find anyone who'll do small jobs like that nowadays.'

'I'll have to send you Brian.'

'Who?'

'His name is Brian Thorpe and he's been doing some work for us – some units for Alice's room, somewhere to put her toys away and get them off the floor. He's basically a carpenter, but he'll turn his hand to anything.'

'Goodness, he sounds too good to be true. How did you find him?'

'Edward recommended him.'

Edward is one of the senior partners in Michael's law firm, as well as a good friend, and I'd take his recommendation on anything.

'Well, I'd certainly be grateful.'

'Oh, Brian's *wonderful!*' Thea said when I was talking to her on the phone next day. 'He's a brilliant workman and so clever. He's made one of the units in Alice's room so that it doubles as a desk for her. She adores it. And he's put up a marvellous corner unit for me in the kitchen – just the right height, and stepped shelves so that you can get twice as much in.'

'He sounds brilliant.'

'Oh, he is,' Thea said earnestly, 'and he clears up after himself splendidly – never a speck of sawdust or anything.'

'There must be something,' I said. 'He can't be that perfect. Does he play Radio One very loudly?'

'Oh no – no radio. I did hear him humming the other day, but quite softly. Oh yes, and he and Alice were singing "Rock a'bye baby" together when he was working in her room.'

'I can't wait!'

When Brian arrived the following week

(the day he said he would and right on time) he was older than I had expected, in his forties probably. He was tall and thin, slightly stooping, his dark hair was going grey and he wore gold-rimmed spectacles so that he looked more like an academic than a carpenter. His voice was quiet and he didn't have the local accent. There was something about him that puzzled me, though I couldn't identify it. His manner was pleasing and he certainly knew what he was talking about.

'I could make you new windows and fit them easily enough,' he said, when he had examined them. 'Though I imagine this is a listed building, so they would have to be identical with these.'

'That's right,' I said. 'How clever of you to have thought of that.'

He smiled. 'I do a lot of work on old houses, restoration and so on. That's the sort of job I prefer.'

'And you could manage the leaded panes all right?'

'Oh yes, that's no problem.'

'That would be wonderful.'

He examined the window frame again.

'I think I could find you some local slate for the sill, if you like. It would be quite in

41

keeping and it wouldn't rot away as the wood has, especially if I angle it slightly. You see how the rain from the thatch drips straight onto the sill.'

'That's a marvellous idea!'

'Right then, I'll just take some measurements then, if that's all right.'

'Of course. Would you like some tea or coffee?'

'Tea would be nice.'

'He's absolutely brilliant,' I told Rosemary when we were having coffee in The Buttery a few days later. 'He really knows what he's doing and he's made some very useful suggestions – for instance, as well as the slate sill I told you about, he's going to move the guttering so that the rainwater doesn't splash down the side of the house like it's done for years. And he's going to redo the back porch so that I have proper shelves for my plants there.'

'He certainly sounds an absolute paragon,' Rosemary said. 'Where does he come from? Is he local?'

'He doesn't sound local, but he lives out at Withycombe. With his mother, apparently.'

'No wife and family?'

'Not that he's mentioned.'

'Divorced, probably, people these days mostly are. Did I tell you that Maureen's daughter has split up with Keith and is back home with the baby?'

'No! But they've only been married for four years.'

'I know. Poor Maureen, she's very upset – she never liked Keith and begged Sandy not to marry him – and Denis is being difficult about the broken nights they're all having because of the baby. Maureen says he should be more supportive of his daughter, but you know what he's like.'

'Oh dear.'

'At least when Colin and Charlotte split up,' Rosemary said, referring to her son and his unhappy marriage, 'there weren't any children.'

'And,' I said soothingly, 'they've both found new partners and seem very happy.'

'It does seem strange,' Rosemary said, 'to have a Canadian daughter-in-law I've never seen.'

'Oh, I expect they'll come over soon.'

'They were coming over straight after the wedding, but then Colin got this new appointment in Montreal and things were a bit hectic.'

'I can't think why you and Jack don't go

over and visit *them*. I believe Montreal is gorgeous.'

'I'd love to – Colin keeps asking us to, but you know what Jack is like about Abroad!'

'Oh dear. *Men!*'

The windows were duly finished and fitted and the polished slate sill was so beautiful I had to keep going out and admiring it. I found Brian an agreeable person as well as a good workman. He was quite prepared to chat over his cups of tea, though always on general topics, never anything personal, but whatever he said was sensible and well considered. He was also very good with the animals, never minding letting Foss in and out of whichever door or window took his fancy.

'Cats know their own minds,' he said, stroking Foss in just the right way along his spine, 'people could learn a lot from cats.'

'How to be selfish!' I said laughing.

'Well, sometimes you have to look out for yourself. No one else will.'

I looked at him in surprise since there was a sharper note in his voice than usual when he made a general statement. But I didn't comment on it, respecting his reserve.

Because he was so reliable I was surprised

44

and then worried when he didn't arrive at his appointed time one morning. Ten o'clock came and then eleven and I was just on the point of ringing him when the telephone rang. Brian's voice was hoarse and strained, almost as if he was whispering.

'I'm very sorry, Mrs Malory,' he said. 'I'm not going to be able to get in to you today.'

'Oh dear, is something the matter?'

'It's Mother – she's not well. I have to stay with her.'

'Yes, of course. Has she seen a doctor?'

'It's all under control...'

He broke off as I heard what sounded like a shout in the background.

'I'm sorry,' he repeated. 'I'll be in as soon as I can.'

'Don't worry,' I said. 'Whenever you can manage...'

My voice trailed away as I heard him put down the phone.

'Do you know anything about Brian's mother?' I asked Thea when I went round there later.

'Not really.'

I explained about Brian's phone call. 'It was a bit odd,' I said. 'His voice was sort of strange and someone seemed to be shouting and he rang off very abruptly, which isn't like him at all.'

'It happened a couple of times when he was working for us,' Thea said, 'the having to stay at home and look after his mother, but I didn't gather what was the matter with her. He didn't say and I didn't ask. You know how you can't really ask him anything personal.'

'I know. Most people are perfectly happy to talk about themselves and their family, but Brian never does.'

'Just as well, perhaps, you know how awful it is when people go on and on and the work never seems to get done!'

'Oh I agree,' I said. 'I suppose it's just perversity that when someone *doesn't* say anything I want to know all about them!'

Alice, who had been pouring water from one doll's teacup to another, suddenly decided to pour the whole lot onto the floor and in the ensuing mopping up the subject was forgotten.

Three days later Brian turned up at his usual time.

'I'm sorry I couldn't get here before,' he said.

'That's fine. No problem – there's no hurry for those shelves, I'm just glad to have

46

them done at all! So how is your mother? Better, I hope.'

'Oh yes, she's fine now. I'll just get that new wood from the van...'

Foss, who had come in from the garden to see who had arrived, weaved round his legs, miaowing loudly, looking for attention. Brian bent down and stroked him.

'Do you have any animals?' I asked.

'We used to have a cat, but that was a while since.'

He turned and went outside. Foss, deciding that since he was indoors he ought to be fed, went into the kitchen and walked about determinedly on the worktop until I opened a tin for him. Tris, hearing the sounds of food dishes being put down, emerged from the hall barking hopefully and was fed in his turn. By the time all this was done, Brian was busy working and the opportunity to ask more questions had gone.

But I was puzzled. As I'd said to Thea, I was curious. The shout I'd heard on the phone hadn't sounded, somehow, like the call of a sick elderly woman calling her son, and the way he'd put the phone down so suddenly – it was all a bit of a mystery.

Brian finished the shelves, and a few other

47

odd jobs that I thought I'd get done while he was there, and departed, having presented me with a very modest bill.

'He really is fantastic,' I said to Michael. 'I do hope he stays around.'

'Oh, I think he's more or less committed to looking after his mother.'

'Do you know what's wrong with her?'

'Not really – it seems to be something that flares up suddenly. Oh, before I forget, Thea says would you like to come for lunch on Sunday? Apparently she's got a new recipe she wants your opinion on.'

The days slipped by, more quickly than they used to I'm sure, and suddenly Anthea appeared at the door with her tray of poppies and her collecting tin and I realised with a shock that we were well into November. Remembrance Day was mercifully dry but misty, the air felt damp and low cloud hung over the hills. Since the heating in St James' is always very notional, I put on my winter coat and wore my gloves. The church was filling up as I arrived and sat in my usual pew. The congregation was elderly, many of the older men wearing neat blazers with regimental badges on the pocket and well polished shoes – something I always find very touching. Sidney Middleton was there and other faces I recognised: Bill Goddard, Fred Pudsey, Ernie Shepherd and other ex-servicemen – fewer every year now. Rosemary and Jack slipped into the pew beside me just before George Lennox, carrying the British Legion standard, led the procession into the church.

'Jack lost the car keys!' Rosemary whispered to me as the organ struck up the first hymn.

'Through all the changing scenes of life...' we sang as we rose to our feet, for most of us our thoughts in the past. Later, in the cold, damp churchyard, as we all stood round the war memorial the vicar spoke the familiar words:

'They shall grow not old, as we that are left grow old...'

I thought of my father, a chaplain on the beaches of Normandy, returned home safely after the war, but dying far too young, the horror of what he had seen still in his mind, and of my brother Jeremy, whose brilliant life was cut short by a sniper's bullet in Cyprus.

'At the going down of the sun and in the
      morning
We will remember them.'

The Last Post echoed in the still air, followed by a silence that, as always, felt almost palpable, broken by the thin notes of Reveille. The poppy wreaths were laid and, one by one, the small crosses, each with its individual poppy placed by loving hands. Then George Lennox took up his standard and the Scouts, the Guides and other uniformed figures marched away, leaving the rest of us to put aside our memories and return, as best we could, to the present.

Jack came up behind me.

'OK. Everybody fit, then?'

I was going back to lunch with Rosemary and Jack, something I did every Remembrance Sunday.

'Oh, Jack, do you mind if I follow you on? I want to have a word with Bill Goddard. I won't be long.'

I made my way back up towards the church where a few people were still lingering.

Bill Goddard was a friend of my parents, a small cheerful man, still brisk and upright in spite of his eighty years. As he saw me he broke away from the group and greeted me.

'Sheila! How nice to see you. Keeping well, I hope. Quite a good turn-out – though not many of us left now. You know Bob Wilson's gone? He died in July.'

'Oh no, I hadn't heard. And Bill, I was so sorry to hear about Vera.'

Vera was Bill's sister-in-law, married to his twin brother Frank, who had died in the war. Bill and his wife Betty had been very good to her and her little boy who was only two when his father was killed.

'It was quite sudden,' Bill said. 'Her heart, apparently. It was a bit of a shock!'

'How awful.'

'Terry, that's her lad, he couldn't get back for the funeral.'

'That's sad. He's in New Zealand, isn't he?'

'That's right. He's hoping to get over sometime, but I don't know when. He's asked me to clear the house and put it on the market.'

'Oh dear, that is a big job, isn't it?'

'Not something I'm looking forward to, I can tell you. Vera was never a one for throwing things away!'

He broke off as Sidney Middleton approached.

'Hello, Sheila, good to see you,' he said. 'Splendid service, wasn't it?'

'Yes, very moving. How are you? Still at Lamb's Cottage, I hope.'

'Yes, still there.'

51

'You stay in your own home,' Bill said. 'Hang on to your independence while you can.'

'Bill's right,' I agreed. 'You're perfectly fit and well. You'd hate to be in a retirement home, you know you would!'

'I'd like to stay where I am, certainly,' Sidney said, 'but I don't want David to have to worry about me. He's got enough on his plate as it is.'

'You've got to think of yourself,' Bill said. 'You can't always be thinking of other people. Ah,' he said, 'here's Betty. I must be off, we're having lunch with the children today and she won't thank me if we keep them waiting.'

He moved away and I said to Sidney, 'Do think very carefully about it, won't you? It's a big step. Once you've sold up your home you can't change your mind!'

He smiled. 'I'll think about it. And thank you, Sheila, for your concern. You're a good friend.'

I put my arm round his shoulder and gave him a little hug.

'You take care of yourself,' I said.

As I went down the slope and turned at the lych gate I looked back and saw him standing quite still where I had left him, a small, somehow gallant figure. I waved, but he didn't see me. I sat in the car for a little while, then I started the engine and drove off to the comfort of the company of my friends.

4

The cold damp weather seemed to go on forever, day after day. As I drove into Taviscombe to do some boring food shopping the countryside looked deeply depressing – the last rags of leaves on the trees said all too clearly that Autumn had gone and there was the whole of Winter to get through before we could hope for Spring again. Only a flock of starlings, dotted about on the telegraph wires looking like notes of music, broke the monotony of the grey sky. On an impulse I drove down to the sea-front, but there too the note was one of melancholy, the sea and sky both merging into a uniform greyness that did nothing to lift the spirits. Even the seagulls were not flying but were huddled on the foreshore, their feathers fluffed out, looking as miserable as I felt.

I got out of the car and stood for a while, hoping that a breeze from off the sea would galvanise me into some sort of cheerfulness, but the air was still and heavy. There were very few people about, just a couple walking their dogs on the beach, and I was just about to return to the car and get on with my shopping when a voice behind me said,

'It's Mrs Malory, isn't it?'

I turned and saw a small figure muffled up in an anorak and scarf.

'Not a very nice day, is it, but then, as I always say, if we waited for a nice day every time we wanted to do something, we'd wait for ever!'

I recognised the flow of words before I identified the face.

'Oh, Mrs Norton,' I said, fishing in my memory for the name. 'How are you? Have you quite settled in?'

'Oh yes, everything's very cosy now. Well, Jim's just got the spare room to decorate, but then, I said to him, there's no need to break your neck getting that done, we're not expecting visitors!'

'You haven't anyone coming for Christmas then?'

'No.' She was silent for a moment. 'It'll be just us. Mind you,' she went on, 'there's always something to do – for instance, I'm not really happy about some of the cupboards in the kitchen. They're a bit high for me, seeing as how I'm just a little one! So that's got to be done and then I was thinking that it would be nice to have a sun lounge built on at the back, leading out of the living room – you know, for plants and things. To be honest with you I'm not much of a gardener (that's Jim's speciality) but I do love my house plants! Jim's put up some shelves for me, but it would be nice to have a sun-lounge as well.'

'You're very lucky to have someone who's so handy about the house,' I said, feeling that some comment was called for.

'Oh, Jim's very good, there's nothing he can't turn his hand to. I was saying to my neighbour the other day – we've got very nice neighbours, a Mr and Mrs Goddard, do you know them? An elderly couple but very nice. Anyway, I was saying to Mrs Goddard, any little job you want doing, just ask, Jim will be only too pleased. Well, I do think we should help each other if we can and they're really quite elderly, as I said.'

'Yes, I do know them,' I said, 'they've lived in Taviscombe all their lives, and so have I.'

'Really! Fancy that! You must all have seen some changes – even in a sleepy little place like this.'

'Yes,' I agreed. 'Things have certainly changed, even in Taviscombe.'

'Well,' she said, 'I must be getting along.

It's been so nice having a chat. Now do drop by if you're passing, we'd love to see you any time.'

Strangely enough this encounter had the effect of cheering me up and I made my way to the supermarket in a much brighter frame of mind.

'How do you feel,' Rosemary asked, 'about a trip to Taunton before it gets all clogged up with Christmas shoppers?'

'Good idea. I want to get a few things for Alice's stocking and there's not much in Taviscombe.'

'Mother wants a Pyrenean wool dressing gown – heaven alone knows if I can find one. I may have to go to Exeter or even Bath, but I thought I'd try Taunton first.'

Amazingly Taunton did yield up the dressing gown, but there was only one and Rosemary wasn't very happy about the colour.

'She did say blue and she's never been very keen on green, especially dark green.'

'Still, it's blissfully soft and warm,' I said. 'And at least you found one.'

'Oh well,' Rosemary said philosophically, 'she was bound to object to *something* about it and it might as well be the colour. Did you get what you wanted?'

'Yes, some dear little tiny furry animals – I long to keep them myself – and some doll's clothes for her baby doll. Oh yes, and I got a really gorgeous pair of very soft leather gloves for Thea, sort of semi-gauntlet, most elegant.'

'Oh, she'll love those. What are you getting for Michael?'

I groaned. 'You know how difficult it is buying things for men! Poor love, he tries so hard to sound grateful when one produces yet another shirt or pullover. Actually, Thea said he wants a new waterproof jacket so I can get that from Ellicombe's. How about Jack?'

'Wasn't it fortunate? His watch has given out just at the right moment, so I can get him a new one. Nothing expensive, he said, because he wants something he can garden in.'

Since Taunton was so crowded we decided to have lunch at a garden centre we passed on our way home. As is the case nowadays, the plants and garden things took up only a fraction of the space, and the general impression was of an enormous craft centre – pottery of every description, hundreds of candles, table mats, wind chimes, sheaves of artificial flowers, stained glass this and that, jars and jars of 'home-made' jams and chutneys – not to mention the vast pet department – hundreds of fleecy dog-beds and cat baskets, great sacks of dried food and cat litter, rubber bones, fluffy mice, collars, leads and medicaments for every imaginable animal ailment. And of course, it being November, there were acres of Christmas decorations, forests of artificial trees and glitter everywhere.

The café which sold tea, coffee and Light Lunches was very full.

'Oh dear,' Rosemary said, 'a Senior Citizens' outing – I thought I saw a minibus in the car park.'

'It's all right,' I said. 'Look, there's a table for two over in that corner. You go and grab it and I'll get the food. Ham sandwich and coffee all right?'

'I suppose,' I said, when we were settled with our sandwiches (cheese and pickle because all the ham had gone) 'that technically *we're* senior citizens.'

'Oh, don't!' Rosemary exclaimed. 'I can't bear it! That's the thing – everyone tells you that the big jump is from youth to middle age, but it isn't at all. The really ghastly one is from middle age to old age. I mean, you trundle along quite happily through your forties and fifties, probably your early sixties too, without feeling much different, then suddenly there are things you can't do, or can only do more slowly or less well. And you know that it's not going to get any better – in fact it's going to get worse!'

'I know. It's a dismal prospect. I try not to think about it. Just live one day at a time, that's what my mother used to say. Anyway, we're not absolutely decrepit yet! And, if you come to think about it, as long as the children and grandchildren need us, we'll still feel useful and that's a marvellous way of keeping real old age at bay!'

'I suppose so,' Rosemary said grudgingly. 'Oh, that reminds me, I promised Jilly that I'd get her some of those special dog biscuits. I know they have them here.'

'You see!' I said. 'They still need us and will go on needing us...'

I broke off.

'What is it?' Rosemary asked.

'It's Brian,' I said. 'You know, the splendid handyman I told you about. He's having lunch here.'

'Why shouldn't he?'

'He's with a woman!'

'So?'

'Well – well, it's just a surprise that's all.'

I tried to cast surreptitious glances at Brian and his companion. For some reason I didn't want him to know that I had seen him. He seemed quite different from the Brian I knew, talking animatedly to the woman. She was small, dark haired and vivacious and they seemed to be very much at ease with each other. After a while they got up to go and I bent down to pick up my handbag so that he wouldn't see me as they passed.

'What was all that about?' Rosemary asked curiously.

'I don't know,' I said. 'But it was so unexpected, not like Brian at all – it almost seemed like a secret assignation.'

'Perhaps she's married.'

'Could be. But – well – that doesn't seem Brian's style.'

'You never know with people,' Rosemary said.

'No,' I agreed. 'You never know.'

Anthea carefully lifted the large cardboard box onto the table and examined the contents.

'We've got a nice lot of jam and some marmalade as well,' she said, 'and I've got the promise of a dozen cakes.' She fixed me with a stern look. 'And of course, Sheila, you will be making two of your fruit cakes.'

I saw Rosemary suppressing a giggle.

'Yes, Anthea,' I said meekly.

We were in the kitchen at Brunswick Lodge preparing for the Christmas Fayre – an appellation much disliked by many but somehow so honoured by tradition that no one ever considered changing it.

'Shall I put the kettle on?' Rosemary asked. 'I think we deserve a cup of tea after all our hard work. How about you, Mr Norton?'

Jim Norton, who was engaged in some electrical work at the far end of the kitchen, said that would be very kind.

'Now then,' Anthea continued, 'that's the Produce stall dealt with. Oh by the way, Marjorie is going to do some of those bay-leaf balls. It's really quite clever, she sticks twigs of bay leaves into a ball of that foam stuff and ties it up with a ribbon. Most attractive, I'm sure they'll go very well. Actually, I'm not sure if they should go on the produce stall – after all, they are made of *herbs* – but perhaps they should go on the Craft stall with Jennifer's dried flower arrangements and the holly wreaths. What do you think?'

'Oh, Crafts, I think, don't you? Anyway, there probably won't be room on the Produce stall, especially if you make all those scones and mince pies.'

'Oh yes,' Rosemary said. 'I forgot to say, Mother says she's sending two of Elsie's Victoria sponges.'

'Oh well,' I said, 'definitely Craft, then.'

We were drinking our tea (Jim Norton didn't join us, preferring, he said, to Get On With Things, though I think it was because he rather disapproved of our female chatter) when the door opened and Bill Goddard came in.

'I thought this is where I'd find you,' he said. 'Is there a cup for me?'

He laid down a large parcel on the table.

'Betty said you might like to have these for the Fair thing.'

He opened the parcel and spread out several tablecloths, some embroidered, some with crocheted lace edging.

'They're beautiful,' Rosemary said. 'Such fine work! Did Betty do them? It's very good of her to send them. I don't think I could have parted with them!'

'No,' Bill said, 'Vera did them. She was a great one for fancy work, always stitching away I suppose it was something to do to pass the time.'

'But don't you want to keep them?' I asked.

'Betty put one of them aside, but, well, we don't use such things any more. A cup of tea in front of the telly at teatime is more our style now.'

'Well, I'm sure someone will be delighted to buy them,' I said. 'It's very kind of you to let us have them.'

I carefully folded the cloths and put them away while Rosemary poured Bill a cup of tea and pushed a plate of biscuits towards him.

'Oh well, I won't say no,' he said, 'though Betty's always on at me to give up sweet things – she's forever reading these articles in the paper saying everything's bad for you. Still, I reckon it's too late now to make a bad day's work good as my old father used to say.'

'So,' I said, 'how are you getting on with clearing out Vera's house?'

Bill sighed. 'It's a job and a half, I can tell you. The stuff she hoarded. The coal shed alone is full of cardboard boxes!'

'Oh dear.'

'Still, we've cleared most of the downstairs,

Betty and me. A lot of the furniture will go to the auction rooms – she had some nice pieces – and most of the china and ornaments too. There's still some of Terry's things in the cupboard on the landing and I don't know what to do with them. It'd cost a fortune to send them out to New Zealand, but I don't just like to throw them away.'

'Still,' I said, 'I expect he'd have taken anything he *really* wanted when he left home.'

'Don't you believe it!' Rosemary said. 'I've still got a mass of things Jilly left behind when she and Roger got married. I've asked her a hundred times what she wants me to do with them but all she says is they haven't any room, so will I keep them.'

'Actually, yes,' I agreed, 'now you come to mention it, Michael's old room is still full of his things and I hardly like to dump them on poor Thea.'

'That's absolutely ridiculous,' Anthea said firmly. 'When Jean and Kathy left I had a real clear-out and anything they hadn't taken I gave to Oxfam or threw away.'

'Anyway,' I said, hastily turning to Bill, 'at least you've made a good start.'

He shook his head. 'There's still all the stuff up in the loft,' he said. 'Boxes of it.'

'Oh dear.'

'I went up there the other day and I couldn't believe the things she'd kept. One thing, though, that was a bit upsetting.' He paused for a moment and then went on. 'When Frank was killed I was away, of course, in the Army, and it was a while until I got back and could see Vera, to know how she was taking it. Well, she'd been in a right old state, so Betty said. Sort of numb, I suppose. But one thing Betty could never understand. A letter had come for Vera, and it must have been the last one Frank wrote to her before he died. Well, she wouldn't open it. Said she couldn't bear it. And that wasn't all. There were several other letters – one from his commanding officer and a couple from one of his friends who was with him – you know, when he was killed. She wouldn't open them either. She must have put them away up in the loft, because that's where I found them, in an old biscuit tin, still unopened.'

'Good heavens,' Rosemary said. 'So have you read them?'

'No, Betty was calling me, said we had to get back for the television repair man.'

'But you will read them?' I asked.

'Oh yes, I think someone ought to. Mind

you, I suppose Terry should have them really but I think I'd better have a look at them before I pass them on to him. There might be something upsetting... Not that he remembers Frank, of course. He was only a baby.'

'It must have been very strange,' I said, 'finding them after all these years.'

'It gave me a bit of a turn,' Bill said slowly, 'to see Frank's handwriting like that.' He drank the last of his tea and put the cup carefully back in the saucer. 'And now we're all dropping off the perch, one by one, and those of us that's left are getting on. I'm lucky, I've got Betty to keep me going, but poor Sidney – I don't know how much longer he can manage on his own.'

'Oh yes, that reminds me,' Anthea said. 'Marjorie says that David is going to take him to see another retirement home this weekend, somewhere down in Cornwall. It's quite a journey so they're going to stay the night at some hotel down there. St Ives, I think she said.'

'But that's so far away!' I exclaimed. 'He won't know anyone there and it's far too far for his friends from Taviscombe to go and visit him.'

'I believe St Ives is very nice,' Anthea said.

'There's a splendid art gallery there, Jean sent me a postcard when she and Ian were there for a holiday.'

'I don't think Sidney is very keen on art,' I said, 'and even if he was it wouldn't make up for being so far away from his family and friends.'

'I expect David wanted him as far away as possible,' Rosemary said, 'so that he wouldn't have to bother with him any more. Typical!'

'Perhaps,' I said hopefully, 'it won't be suitable in some way. I think it's such a shame that he has to move out of Lamb's Cottage, it must have so many memories for him.'

'He will take his memories with him,' Rosemary said gently.

'We all have to move on, Sheila,' Anthea said. 'After all, we're none of us getting any younger.'

And really, I thought, as I gathered up the cups and saucers and rinsed them in the sink, there's no answer to that.

5

It was over a week later that I finally got down to making the fruit cakes for the Christmas Fayre. As I got out the ingredients, the scales and the mixing bowl, Tris materialised at my feet. He is passionately fond of sultanas and seems to know, as if by magic, when I am about to be using them. Foss was in his usual position, sitting on top of the microwave, where he is able to command a good overview of what's happening in the kitchen and where he can bat at my hair with his paw when I pass to remind me of his continued presence.

While I had the things out, I thought I'd make a sponge and a few scones to put in the freezer to have by me in case anyone called. After all that, though, I didn't really feel like cooking lunch so I made myself a poached egg on toast and was just sitting down to have it when the phone rang. It was Michael.

'Hello, Ma. I thought I'd better let you know. Sidney's dead.'

'Oh no! What happened? Was it a heart attack?'

'They don't know yet – there's got to be a post mortem.'

'How awful!'

'Mrs Harrison found him when she went in to clean.'

'Oh dear, poor Sidney, dying all alone like that. Perhaps it would have been better if David *had* got him into a home.'

'Perhaps.'

'How did you hear about it?'

'We're his solicitors. David got in touch.'

'How dreadful for Mrs Harrison. She must have had a terrible shock.'

'Yes. Look, Ma, I must go. I've got an appointment in a few minutes, but I just thought you'd want to know...'

'Yes, of course. Do let me know if you hear anything else.'

I went back to my poached egg, but it was cold and congealed and, anyway, I didn't really feel like eating anything so I just made myself a cup of tea and sat thinking about Sidney.

'Oh, isn't that sad!' Rosemary said when I rang her later.

'He looked so well when I saw him at the

Remembrance Day service,' I said. 'A bit frail, but it was a cold, miserable day.'

'I didn't know he had a heart condition, did you?' Rosemary asked.

'We don't know that it was heart. Michael said there'd have to be a post mortem.'

'How did Michael hear?'

'David rang because they're Sidney's solicitors.'

'Typical of David!' Rosemary said. 'Thinking about the money, I suppose.'

'Well, to be fair, I suppose they had to know. But I expect he's keen to know about the money.'

'Sidney must have been pretty well off. They say he made a packet when he worked in the City. And with property prices as they are Lamb's Cottage must be worth a lot, too. There's quite a bit of land as well as the house.'

'Oh yes, it's a lovely spot. I expect with all that money David will be able to send those boys of his to an even grander public school!'

But when I ran into Bridget a few days later she had quite different news. I was taking a short cut through the park when I ran into her, walking her dog.

'Bridget,' I said, 'I was so sorry to hear

about poor Sidney.'

'Yes, it was very sad.'

'You'll miss him.'

'Well...' She hesitated. 'To be honest, I didn't see that much of him. David went round there quite a lot, of course, but he didn't visit us all that often.'

'When is the funeral?'

'We don't know yet. David will put a notice in the *Free Press* and the *Telegraph* when we do.'

'Will the boys come back for it?'

'Oh no, David thinks it might be upsetting for them.'

'I suppose they didn't see that much of Sidney, either,' I said, 'being away at school...'

'Oh, Sheila!' Bridget interrupted me. 'Such good news! They're coming home at the end of term – they're not boarding any more. They'll be day boys at Taunton School.'

Her eyes were shining and she looked positively animated.

'That's lovely for you, Bridget,' I said. 'I know how much you missed them. But I thought David was frightfully keen on boarding school, meeting all the right sort of boys and so on. What made him change his mind?'

'Oh, I think he was missing them, too, and he knew how much I wanted them at home.'

'Well, that's splendid,' I said. 'It's good to hear something nice at a sad time like this.'

I bent and patted the spaniel which was whining softly, annoyed at having his walk interrupted. 'We were all very shocked to hear about Sidney. I had no idea he had a heart condition.'

'Oh, it wasn't a heart attack.'

'Oh. I suppose I just assumed it must be, since it was so sudden. What was it, then?'

'The post mortem said it was carbon monoxide poisoning.'

'What!'

'That's what they said.'

'But how...?'

'They think it was something to do with the stove. I'm afraid I don't really know the details. Oh dear,' she went on as the spaniel began to pull at its lead, 'Dandy wants to be off. Goodbye Sheila. I expect I'll see you at the funeral.'

'Yes,' I said, 'I expect you will.'

'I couldn't believe it,' I said to Thea, when I went round there later. 'She just came out with it, almost like an afterthought. Well, not even that really. In fact, if I hadn't said that about a heart attack I don't believe she'd have mentioned it at all!'

'Good heavens!'

'I mean, I know she's a bit vague – not to say dim! – but you would have thought that would have been the first thing she would have told me.'

'Carbon monoxide poisoning, that's terrible,' Thea said. 'I wonder how long it was before Mrs Harrison found him? She doesn't go in every day, does she?'

'Oh, don't! I can't bear to think of him lying there for days.'

'I expect he just drifted away, just became unconscious. I don't imagine he suffered. It's not like smoke, you don't choke or anything.'

'Still. If he'd been discovered soon enough he might not have died. They could have taken him to hospital, given him oxygen, things like that.'

'Bridget didn't say anything about that?' Thea asked.

'No, all she wanted to talk about was the boys being taken out of boarding school.'

'I expect she was really thrilled about that.'

'Oh yes, she was. And that's another

peculiar thing. Why has David suddenly decided to bring them home? I can't believe he did it to please her!'

'Perhaps he was missing them, too?'

'That's what Bridget said, but that doesn't seem like David. From what I can gather he didn't spend much time with them when they *were* at home. And I know that Sidney was sad that he didn't get to see much of them. Oh dear, *poor* Sidney! I really am upset about him. I do wish we knew what happened.'

'Perhaps Michael will know a bit more.'

We were unable to continue this conversation since Alice, newly awoken from her afternoon nap, demanded our presence at the seemingly never-ending dolls' tea-party that currently occupied most of her waking moments.

'There's not much more that I can add,' Michael said when he rang that evening. 'There was a post mortem and they established that he died of carbon monoxide poisoning. There'll have to be an inquest, to see what caused it, though it seems most likely to be that stove. He always sat in the kitchen in the evenings, of course, and that's where Mrs Harrison found him.'

'Did they say how long he'd been dead?'

'They said about a day – well, two nights and a day, presumably.'

'How awful! If only someone had gone in the morning after it happened they might have saved him.'

'I don't know. He was old and a bit bronchial, anyway. It probably wouldn't have made any difference.'

'Did Mrs Harrison notice anything? I mean, what about the fumes when she went in?'

'She had no idea – thought it was a heart attack, like we all did. The stove had gone out by then, of course, been out for quite a while, so the fumes had more or less dissipated, and anyway there was no smell or smoke or anything.'

'How horrible. No wonder they call carbon monoxide poisoning the silent killer!'

'He should have had one of those alarms. We all should, really I'm going to get some for us and I'll get a couple for you, shall I?'

'Oh yes, please. I do sometimes have a fire in the sitting-room now the weather's so dismal. Which reminds me, I must get Reg to come and sweep the chimney before I light it again.'

Reg Burnaby is our local chimney sweep

and general handyman – he's brilliant at dealing with old and difficult chimneys, but that's not the only reason why his services are so much in demand. He is an inveterate gatherer and general clearing house for news and gossip throughout the district. If anyone knew more details about Sidney's death I was quite sure it would be Reg.

When I was a child 'having the sweep in' was a major and unpleasant operation. All the smaller items of furniture had to be huddled into the centre of the room and covered up, the larger pieces were likewise swathed in dust-sheets, while the grate and the surrounding hearth was cleared of all impedimenta and still more cloths put down. After it was all over, after the brushes had been pushed up the chimney and appeared satisfactorily poking through the top, there was much sweeping up and a fine film of grime clung to all the fittings while the acrid, unmistakable smell of soot hung in the air for what seemed like weeks afterwards. It's all quite different now, of course, it's all done with vacuums and such like and you really don't have to cover anything up at all. Reg did the job in no time and then, as always, he washed his hands at the sink and we both settled down at the kitchen table with a large pot of tea and some shortbread biscuits (his favourites) while he prepared to fill me in on all the local news.

I didn't even have to raise the subject of Sidney's death since it was obviously at the forefront of his mind.

'A dreadful thing about Mr Middleton, then,' he said, spooning sugar into his cup and stirring it vigorously. 'I can't understand it at all.'

'About the stove being faulty?' I asked.

'There wasn't nothing wrong with that there stove,' he said firmly. 'I checked 'un myself not three weeks ago, took 'un all to pieces and did a proper job.'

'Really?'

'*And* the chimney too. Clean and sweet as a nut that chimney were, and folks have no right to go saying otherwise!'

'You cleaned the chimney as well?'

'That I did. Cleaned 'un proper, same as I always do.'

'How extraordinary. But then, if it wasn't the stove or the chimney, what on earth could have caused it?'

'That I couldn't say, but there's no call to go blaming that stove or that chimney and so I'd tell anyone who asked.'

'Have the police spoken to you? I expect they've got to investigate it.'

'That Bob Lister, police *sergeant* he calls himself now, he come round to see me and I told him what I've just told you and he says I've got to tell it to that there coroner at this inquest they'm having.'

'Oh yes,' I said, refilling his cup, 'I heard there was going to be one. But it's all very odd.'

'You may well say there's something odd about it,' Reg said, waving his teaspoon to emphasise his point. 'If that stove and that chimney wasn't to blame – and I'd take my bible oath as they wasn't – then there's only one way of looking at it.'

'What's that?' I asked.

'Then it wasn't no accident. Someone did it a'purpose.'

'But how could anyone?'

'There's ways of doing things.'

'But who on earth would *want* to do such a thing? I mean – Sidney was the sweetest man, everyone loved him.'

'That's as maybe. Folks will talk.'

'What are they saying?'

But Reg proved unexpectedly uncommunicative and, finishing up his tea and taking the remaining handful of biscuits

('Didn't get no breakfast'), he departed, leaving me puzzled and confused.

'You mean,' Rosemary said, 'that he was implying that Sidney was killed *deliberately?* Surely not. Everyone liked him so much!'

'I agree, it's pretty unlikely. But, then, if Reg really did take the stove to pieces and sweep the chimney – and Reg is totally reliable about any job he does – then how *could* Sidney have died of carbon monoxide poisoning?'

'But he did.'

'That's what the post mortem said. Perhaps the inquest will make it a bit clearer.'

But the inquest, perhaps because of Reg's evidence or maybe for other reasons – I didn't go myself so I didn't hear the details – was adjourned for further enquiries.

'Whatever that may mean,' I said to Rosemary. 'Still, it does mean they can go ahead with the funeral. Are you and Jack going?'

'Jack can't, he's got to be in Bristol that day. So shall we go together?'

Rosemary and I were waiting our turn to go into the church, while Chris Brown from the local paper was taking the names of people there for his report, when Ernie

Shepherd and Fred Pudsey came up behind us.

'Dreadful thing about Sidney,' Fred said. 'Damned stupid way to go.'

'I know,' I said. 'It's awful. He'll be greatly missed.'

'Still,' Fred said, looking at the queue of people in front of us with some satisfaction, 'we're giving him a good send-off, quite a decent turn-out.'

'That's true,' I agreed. 'Is Bill coming?'

'I didn't speak to him myself but Betty said he couldn't make it,' Fred said. 'Which is a pity. There are not so many of us left.'

Still, the church was full. As well as the old friends from his schooldays and from his days in the army there were many others, younger friends, who had only known him since he had come back from London when he retired.

'I'm so glad there are a nice lot of people,' Rosemary said, looking round the church. 'It's always so sad when there's only a handful of relations and nobody else.'

The organist, who had been playing very softly something vaguely Elgarish, struck up a voluntary as the coffin with its single wreath was carried into the church, followed by the vicar with David and Bridget walking slowly behind him. David looked very pale and strained, more upset than I thought he would be. Bridget looked nervous and uncertain and David had to take her by the arm and lead her into the right pew.

It was a good traditional service with the 23rd Psalm, a reading from *Pilgrim's Progress* and 'The Day Thou Gavest Lord is Ended' (which always makes me cry), the sort of service that Sidney would have liked. I gave David full marks for that.

'I don't really want to go to the cemetery, do you?' Rosemary said as the coffin was carried out and people began to disperse.

'No, I don't think so. Come back with me and have some tea.'

As I got up to go I turned and looked round and to my surprise, at the back of the church, still sitting in his pew, I saw Brian.

'I'll see you outside,' I said to Rosemary. 'There's someone I want to have a word with.'

I walked up to where Brian was sitting and said, 'Hello. I didn't know you knew Sidney. It was good of you to come.'

He looked at me blankly and, for a moment, I thought he hadn't recognised me. Then he slowly got to his feet.

'I came,' he said, and his voice was cold

and expressionless, 'to make sure that the old devil was really dead.'

He moved past me down the aisle and was gone.

6

'I simple couldn't *believe* it,' I said to Rosemary for the umpteenth time. 'I mean, what an extraordinary thing to say at a funeral, and about someone like Sidney!'

'Very odd,' Rosemary agreed. 'Was he all right? I mean, he wasn't ill or anything?'

'No, he seemed perfectly normal. That is, he looked very white and strained.' I picked up another scone and buttered it. 'I mean, I didn't even know that he *knew* Sidney.'

'Perhaps he did some work for him and there was a disagreement.'

'I suppose,' I said doubtfully. 'But even so, it's a pretty extreme thing to say about any-one. And,' I continued as I spooned the jam into a dish, 'it's so unlike Brian. He's always seemed to be to be such a mild-mannered man, you know, quiet and reserved.'

'Oh well,' Rosemary said, 'people do behave oddly at funerals. I remember Milli-cent Edwards making very loud derogatory remarks about Cousin Ian all through the vicar's address at *his* funeral.'

'At least she was a relation.'

'Talking of relations,' Rosemary said, 'I thought David looked quite ill, and as for Bridget, well, I thought at one moment she was going to faint.'

'Yes, that was odd, wasn't it? I really didn't think either of them was particularly fond of Sidney, in fact I'm sure David wasn't, and Bridget told me just the other day that she didn't really know him that well.'

'Well, as I say, funerals affect people in funny ways. I must say, this jam is delicious. What is it?'

'Raspberry and gooseberry – the gooseberries help it to set. Straining the raspberries is a bit of a bore but I can't manage the pips nowadays!'

'I know,' Rosemary agreed. 'They're all right in fresh raspberries, it's when they're cooked they get all hard and wooden.' She spread jam on another scone. 'I suppose David will sell Lamb's Cottage. I mean, I don't expect they'd want to live in it. Unless, if the boys are coming home, they might want to keep horses and there is that big paddock.'

'I wouldn't think so, really. David's work's in Taunton and Lamb's Cottage is the wrong side of Taviscombe, so that would add miles to his journey every day. If they wanted more land they'd probably buy something in the Quantocks.'

Michael confirmed that the house was being put up for sale.

'It's a very peculiar will,' he said.

'Really? In what way?'

'Sidney didn't leave anything at all to David.'

'What!'

'Apart from a few minor legacies and one other bequest, everything goes into a Trust for the boys.'

'Good heavens. No wonder David looked so peculiar at the funeral!'

'Sidney left a few antiques to Dick and Marjorie Croft – you know, his friends in the village. And he left you that little Victorian table inlaid with mother of pearl, the one you always admired so much.'

'Oh, that was kind!'

'I thought you'd be pleased.'

'And what about the other bequest? You did say there was another one, didn't you?'

'Oh yes, and that's the most peculiar thing of all. He left a cottage in Withycombe – Rose Cottage – together with quite a large sum of money, to an Emily Thorpe.'

It took a moment for me to make the connection.

'Withycombe? Thorpe? You don't mean...'

'Brian's mother.'

'But why?'

'Your guess is as good as mine.'

'So that's the connection...' I began. Then I told Michael about Brian's strange remark at the funeral. 'So,' I said, 'there must have been something pretty nasty going on somewhere.'

'You're right. Definitely peculiar. But – well – not the sort of thing you'd associate with someone like Sidney!'

'Did *you* draw up the will? Did you know about all this?'

'No, Sidney was Edward's client, so I had no idea. But Edward's had to go to Spain to sort out some property deal, and he left me to deal with the probate and so on.'

'Didn't Edward think it was all a bit odd?'

'No, not really. As far as he was concerned it was just a business arrangement. And if you didn't actually know Sidney you wouldn't think much of it. After all, people set up Trusts and make slightly odd bequests all the time.'

'It must have been something really awful,' I said, reverting to my earlier theme.

'Brian sounded so bitter. And there's this odd thing about his mother, too. Something very strange there, don't you think? How many middle-aged men live with their mothers these days anyway?'

'Well, if she's ill...'

'And what *sort* of illness is it? That time I rang him up, I heard someone shouting in the background.'

'Oh, come on! You're not thinking mad women in attics like the woman in that book?'

'The first Mrs Rochester. No, well, perhaps nothing as dramatic as that, but peculiar all the same.'

'Anyway,' Michael said, 'I've given the pieces they were left to Dick and Marjorie. I know we haven't got probate yet, but I think it's safer if the cottage is being left empty until it's sold. So would you like to come and collect your table?'

'Of course. When?'

'Tomorrow's Saturday, so how about then? About eleven o'clock suit you? Mrs Harrison said she'd come about eleven-thirty to give me her set of keys.'

Lamb's Cottage didn't have that stale, shut-up smell that empty houses sometimes have. I remarked on this to Michael.

'Oh well, it all had to be thoroughly aired out after the carbon monoxide, and then Mrs Harrison's been coming in to keep an eye on things so the heating's been left on.'

It was all right in the sitting room. I'd hardly ever sat in there with Sidney in recent years so it didn't feel strange without him.

'I'd better have a quick look round,' Michael said, 'to see that everything is all right.'

He went upstairs and I went into the kitchen to wait for him. It was different there. With no Sidney it seemed a bleak and miserable place. It was colder, too, than the rest of the house. The woodburning stove looked dead and somehow sinister – I could almost persuade myself that I felt a chill emanating from it. Some of the plants had dropped their leaves and they lay in untidy heaps on the windowsill. The china on the dresser no longer shone and the screen of the television standing there looked like a blank, expressionless face. Worse of all, the calendar still displayed the picture and the name of the month before, a reminder that no one would now turn the page as the days went by.

Somehow I couldn't bring myself to sit down, so I went over to the window and stood looking out at the dismal winter landscape. The garden was tidy but the monochrome of browns and greys and blacks – the soil of the empty flower beds, the bare branches of the trees – was depressing. The hills beyond the garden, wreathed in mist and low cloud, added to the melancholy of the scene. The door behind me opened and a voice said,

'Oh, Mrs Malory, you did give me a turn, standing there like that!'

'I'm so sorry, Mrs Harrison. I didn't hear you arrive. I was just thinking how sad everything looks.'

'Sad isn't the word, really shocking! Such a dreadful thing to happen to poor Mr Middleton. I still haven't got over it!'

'It must have been awful for you, finding him like that.'

'Oh, it was dreadful. My John said I was white as a sheet when I got back home. To tell the truth, I'm still not right.'

'Was it the carbon monoxide?' I asked. 'Did it get to you?'

'Well, no,' she said reluctantly, 'it had more or less gone by then. That's why,' she went on, warming to her theme, 'I didn't know what had happened to *him*. Lying there in his chair he was, just as though he was fast asleep. He looked really peaceful. There now, I thought, he's just slipped away. Well, he was quite an age, wasn't he?'

'What did you do?'

'I rang Dr Macdonald. He's my doctor as well as Mr Middleton's, so I know him quite well – he was really good when my Jason had that motorcycle accident and broke his collarbone – and he came at once.'

'And what did he say?'

'I could tell that he was puzzled – not that I was there when he saw to Mr Middleton, of course – but he came and told me that there'd have to be – a what do you call it? – an examination of the body...'

'A post mortem?'

'That's it. Seems there's a law or something when people die suddenly. Anyway, he asked if I had Mr David's number and he rang him. Well, he wasn't there, at work of course, but he left a message with his wife and Mr David had to make all the arrangements. I saw you at the funeral, a lovely service, wasn't it? I thought the vicar spoke really well.'

'Yes. It was very moving.'

'I thought there might have been a flag on

the coffin, him having been in the war. When my uncle Sam died he was in the army too – there was a Union Jack on the coffin and a lovely wreath in the shape of his regimental badge.'

'Fancy,' I said.

'It was really queer, though,' she went on. 'They say there must have been something wrong with the chimney because Reg – you know Reg – had that stove to pieces not long since and it was drawing beautifully. Well, I know that because I came in and lit it myself the day he got back from Cornwall with Mr David. Nothing wrong with it then.'

'And that was the evening when...'

'When he passed away. It's a real mystery. They think it must be something to do with the chimney – I don't understand these things – but I do know Reg swept that chimney when he saw to the stove.'

'Perhaps it was a bird's nest,' I suggested. 'Jackdaws, perhaps. They build in chimneys, don't they?'

She looked at me pityingly. 'Not in November they don't.'

'No, of course not, how silly of me. But I can't imagine what else it could have been.'

'That's what I said to my John. I can't think *what* it could have been.'

'The inquest was adjourned,' I said, 'so I suppose they're still looking into things.'

'Well, I don't see how they can tell anything about what happened *now*. I mean, if there wasn't anything to show straight away, they're not likely to find anything now, are they?'

I had to agree that it didn't seem likely.

'It's going to seem queer not coming in here any more,' she said, looking around. 'I've been with Mr Middleton a long time, ever since his poor wife died, and that was some years now. I suppose everything will go. I mean, I don't expect Mr David will want anything, I believe he has a lovely home. But it's a funny feeling to think of all the things you've looked after and polished and kept nice, going to be sold in some auction place. Sad really.'

We were both silent for a moment in tribute to this thought.

'Right. I think that's everything,' Michael said then, coming into the room. 'Thank you so much, Mrs Harrison, for seeing to things, it's been a great help. The house won't be going onto the market immediately so I'll keep the central heating on just in case the weather gets colder and we have a bad frost.'

Mrs Harrison fished in her handbag and produced a bunch of keys.

'Here you are, then. All the keys are there. That big one is for the mortice on the front door and that little one there is for the padlock on the woodshed.' She looked round the room once again. 'The end of an era, you might say. Well, I must be getting along. You know where I am, if you need me for anything.'

When she had gone I, too, looked round the kitchen. Another of my mother's generation gone. Here, in these familiar surroundings, it seemed to hit me more strongly than it had at the funeral. And with the death of another of her friends it seemed somehow that I had lost a little bit more of her.

'Are you all right, Ma?' Michael asked anxiously.

I pulled myself together. 'Yes, I'm fine. Just a bit melancholy.'

'I'll lock the front door,' Michael said, 'and we'll go out the back. I'd better check on the outbuildings as we go.'

As we walked round the side of the house Michael stopped and looked up at the chimney, then his gaze travelled down onto the wall of the house.

'Yes, well, Reg *did* sweep the chimney, like he said. Look, you can see where the soot has spilt out when he had the inspection plate off.'

He pointed to a metal plate let into the wall. Below it there were streaks of soot caught in the rough sandstone surface of the wall.

'What's that?' I asked.

'It's the inspection plate. You can take it off and get to the chimney from here. I expect Reg swept the chimney from the outside to save making a mess in the house.'

'How does it work?'

'It's quite simple. The chimney flue divides inside – sort of a Y shape – and one arm goes up the chimney proper and one arm comes out here. It's usually done when the stove is installed.'

'What a good idea...' I looked at the plate. It was about ten inches square with a slot – the sort you could open with a coin or a screwdriver – at one side. 'It's very neat,' I said, 'and quite unobtrusive. Could I have one fitted on my chimney? It would be lovely to be able to have it swept with absolutely no disruption inside.'

'I don't see why not. You'd better ask Reg what he thinks. Here are the keys of the

Land Rover. You go and get in while I have a quick look round out here. I've put the table in the back.'

The table, oval-shaped mahogany with a design of flowers executed in delicate mother of pearl, looked immediately at home under the sitting-room window. I drew Rosemary's attention to it when she called the following day.

'Oh, that *is* pretty. I do love those things. Great Aunt Amy had some lovely pieces but when she died Mother got rid of them all. Her generation despised anything Victorian.'

'I know,' I said, 'it was the same with buildings. All that lovely municipal Gothic torn down after the war and hideous modern stuff put up instead.'

'So is Sidney's furniture to be sold off?'

'He left a few things to the Crofts – you know, Dick and Marjorie, they live in the village and used to do shopping for him and things like that. Otherwise it was a very peculiar will.'

'Really?'

'Nothing at all for David and a Trust set up for the boys. And...' I paused for dramatic effect, 'and a cottage at Withycombe and a substantial sum of money – I quote Michael – left to Brian Thorpe's mother.'

'No!'

'It's true.'

'But why?'

'There is one explanation,' I said, 'but I honestly can't believe it.'

'You mean...?'

'That Mrs Thorpe – or perhaps she isn't Mrs – was Sidney's mistress and Brian is his son.'

'No. No, it can't be. Not Sidney!'

'I agree. It sounds impossible. But what other reason could there be?'

Rosemary shook her head. 'I don't know. I can't think of anything.'

'You see,' I said, 'it would explain, in a way, that extraordinary remark Brian made after the funeral.'

'I suppose so. But still...'

'I know. It simply doesn't fit in with the Sidney we knew.'

We were both silent for a moment, then Rosemary said, 'Of course, there is another possibility.'

'What?'

'It's just possible,' she said slowly, 'that he wasn't the person we thought he was and we didn't know Sidney at all.'

7

I was walking past the houses on the quay when I saw Reg unloading some gear from his van. As he emerged he saw me and said, "Morning Mrs Malory.'

'Oh, Reg,' I said, 'just the person I want to see. You haven't sent me your bill yet. Could you let me have it so I can get it settled before Christmas.'

'Right you are. I'll get onto it tonight.'

'That's good. Oh, and there was something else. Would it be possible for me to have one of those inspection plate things on the wall so that you could get at the chimney from the outside. I was up at Lamb's Cottage a few days ago and I saw that Sidney had one. It seems like a good idea.'

'No reason why you shouldn't. I'll come and have a look next time I'm passing. Up at Lamb's Cottage, was you? I suppose they'm going to sell it. I don't see that son of his wanting to live there. Mind you, it'll fetch a pretty penny these days. I daresay,' he continued, his voice heavy with scorn, 'some off-comer's going to buy it for a fancy price for a second home! It's a disgrace. Didn't ought to be allowed.'

'I know, it's awful, isn't it.'

'My Les, he's having to move away – can't afford to buy anything round here. Mr Middleton, he was going to see if he could hear of something – maybe a council house or a cottage to let – but no hopes of that now.'

'It was very sad. Such a dreadful accident. Have they any idea at all of how it happened? I know you checked the stove for him and, when I was at Lamb's Cottage, I saw by the soot around the inspection plate that you'd swept the chimney.'

Reg, who had been lifting a box of tools from the back of the van, put them down and stared at me.

'No, that's not right,' he said. 'I never swep 'un from the outside. Not when I had the stove to pieces – I did 'un from inside...' His voice trailed away and he looked at me sharply.

'You sure you saw soot all round the plate?'

'Yes,' I said. 'It was caught in the stone work – you know how rough sandstone is – and had dribbled down below.'

Reg was silent for a moment, then he said slowly, 'So that's how they did do it.'

'Who did what?' I asked, puzzled.

'Them as killed Mr Middleton. I knowed *I* had that chimney clear. I thought as how it might have been wet paper or wet rag pushed up the chimney, like. But no, all they had to do was take the plate off.'

'What do you mean?'

'Well, if the plate is off, they fumes can't go up the chimney, they'm going to come back into the room, aren't they?'

'Are they?'

'That's what happened, sure as I'm standing here.' He took off his cap and scratched his head. 'Well I'm damned! Who'd have thought they'd think of that!'

'But Reg,' I said, 'who do you mean – who would have wanted to kill Mr Middleton?'

'I can't say,' he replied cautiously, 'but where there's money – well, you know as how folks talk.'

'You mean David? No, really, I can't believe that. And anyway, he didn't inherit anything himself – it went to the boys.'

'Is that so?' Reg looked at me intently, obviously registering this piece of gossip. 'Still, he was killed no matter who did it.'

'So, will you tell the police?'

His face lightened with pleasure. 'Aye, I'll tell that *Sergeant* Bob Lister. He was so sure it were an accident. Didn't believe me about the stove. Now he'll have to do something about it whether he likes it or not!'

'Yes, well, you must tell someone. After all they adjourned the inquest, didn't they? They must have thought it needed investigating further.'

'That it does...'

He broke off as a woman came out from the house and called to him, 'Reg, are you coming in? Your tea's going cold!'

He picked up his tool-box and closed the back door of the van. 'I told them,' he said triumphantly, 'that it weren't no accident,' and went into the house.

When Michael came round that evening to put a new washer on the tap in the kitchen, I told him what Reg had said.

'Good heavens! He's quite sure?'

'You know Reg. If he said he swept that chimney from inside then he did. And someone must have been doing *something* to that plate fairly recently, because the soot was still there.'

'That's true.' He took a wrench out of his tool bag. 'Have you turned the water off?'

'Yes, of course,' I said impatiently. 'And if someone *had* wanted to kill Sidney, then they could easily have come and blocked off that chimney from the outside. They didn't have to get into the house at all!'

'Just look at that!' Michael said, holding up the old washer. 'Completely perished. I can't imagine why it hasn't gone before.'

'But you do see,' I persisted, 'how simple it would be. You could open that plate with a coin. In the dark! Someone could have come at night, taken off the plate and then, early the next morning, he could have nipped back and screwed it back on again, and no one would have been the wiser.'

Michael carefully slipped the new washer into place and replaced the tap. 'There now,' he said, 'just turn the water back on and we'll see if it's all right.'

I bent down to turn the stop-cock under the sink. 'It's perfectly clear to me that that's how it must have happened,' I said. 'There, how's that?'

Michael turned the tap on. 'That's fine.'

I began to replace the bottles of fabric softener, detergent, and washing up liquid, slightly rusty sprays of polish, air freshener and oven cleaner, together with the old cleaning rags, brushes and pot-scourers that lived in some squalor in the cupboard under the sink. 'I really must clear this lot out sometime,' I said. 'So what do you think?'

'What do I think?'

'About *Sidney!*'

'Oh yes, well, there's certainly something peculiar going on there. But murder? It's a bit drastic. Who would want to kill Sidney?'

I switched the kettle on and got out the cups and tea pot. 'Well, there's Brian, for one. I told you what he said after the funeral. He certainly seemed to hate him. And then being left the cottage and that money...'

'Mm. Could be. But can you really see Brian killing someone?'

'Well, yes,' I said. 'I think I can. Quite reserved, you never know what he's thinking. And *so* bitter! Whatever the reason, he really did sound as if he hated Sidney. Yes, I could imagine him killing someone he hated as much as that.'

'Possibly.'

I got the fruit cake out of the tin. 'Will you have a piece of this, or will it spoil your supper? Here, help yourself.'

Michael cut a hefty slice and said, 'Well, Reg is going to tell the police, you said. We'll have to leave it to them.'

'I don't have much faith in Sergeant Lister, especially since he and Reg seem to have some sort of feud going. Do you think I ought to tell Roger about it?' Roger Eliot is our local Chief Inspector, now based in Taunton, but married to Jilly, Rosemary's daughter and my god-daughter, and still living in Taviscombe. 'I run into him quite often in the town and I could mention it to him casually.'

Michael gave a short laugh, slightly impeded by cake crumbs. 'I know your idea of casual, and so does Roger. Still, if you've got the bit between your teeth over this – and I can see you have – I don't suppose anything I can say will stop you. Is there another cup left in the pot?'

I didn't run into Roger and when I mentioned to Rosemary that I hadn't seen him around she said that he was off on a course.

'Whatever that may mean,' she said. 'Surely there weren't so many courses when we were young, were there? And everyone seemed to manage perfectly well without them. I know Jilly's very fed up about this one. He's up in London for a fortnight and the poor girl's having to do all the Christmas stuff herself. He may not even be back in time for Delia's Nativity play and she's going to be the Angel Gabriel this year.'

'How splendid.'

'Well, yes and no. Delia's thrilled of course, but poor Jilly's got to manufacture an enormous pair of angel's wings out of *something!*' She looked at me curiously. 'Did you want to see Roger about something special?'

I told her what Reg had said. 'I'm sure Sergeant Lister will report it and all that. It's just that – well, since it's Sidney, I did want to see what Roger thought about it all.'

'Yes, I do agree. And do you believe Brian *might* have had something to do with it?'

'I really don't know. I'd hate to think so. He seems such a nice, *genuine* sort of person, but then you never know what someone might be capable of if the provocation was great enough.'

'If Sidney was his father, you mean, and Brian thought his mother had been treated badly?'

'Yes. Though Sidney did leave her the cottage and I suppose he'd let her live there rent free before. Oh really!' I broke off. 'I simply can't *imagine* Sidney living that sort of double life. I mean, he was devoted to Joan.'

'The most unexpected people do have secret lives.'

'But he was so – well, so *nice!*'

Rosemary laughed. 'How do we know? He may have been nice to us, but horrible to other people.'

'But he was such a gentle person. Think how David bossed him around and how well he took it – always saying that David only had his interest at heart when David was badgering him to go into an old people's home.'

'True. But, as I said before, how do we know what he was really like? And there's no way of finding out now.'

Still, I did think I might get some sort of answer from Bridget when I met her in the supermarket a few days later. I thought she was looking rather drawn and strained, not at all well, in fact, but I greeted her cheerfully.

'How are you?' I asked. 'Are you ready for Christmas?'

She gave a tight little laugh. 'Is one ever! No, I'm just rushing round to get as much done as I can before the boys come home. There's been such a lot to do, I'm really behindhand.'

'Yes, of course. And I suppose, in a way, you and David won't be feeling very festive – what with poor Sidney...'

'No.'

'I gather David's putting the house on the market. That's always a bit of a business, isn't it? And I suppose there's no point in trying to do anything in that line before Christmas. It must be a very difficult time for David altogether.' She looked at me sharply and I went on, 'All that business of the inquest being adjourned and everything left in the air like that.'

'Yes,' she said. 'It was unfortunate.'

It seemed a strange choice of words.

'I imagine they have to investigate these things pretty thoroughly,' I said. 'If there's some doubt that it was an accident.' She gave me a frightened look but made no comment. 'I believe Reg – you know Reg Burnaby who does the chimneys and so forth – has some new information that the police are looking at. But I expect you know.'

'I don't know. David may have heard – I believe there was something. I don't really... Look, I'm sorry I have to go. I'm – I'm expecting a phone call... Goodbye.'

She turned her trolley round abruptly and made for the nearest checkout.

'I'm sure she didn't get half the things she wanted,' I said to Rosemary when we met for coffee a little later. 'I did feel rather mean cornering her like that. It was a bit like tormenting a kitten, but I did want to know what was going on there and how much David knew. I think it's quite likely that the police have been talking to him again. She looked very nervy and miserable – I'm sure there's something up there.'

'You don't think just the business about the will?' Rosemary asked. 'I mean, they must have been sure that Sidney would leave everything to them.'

'They're perfectly well off, and the money *is* going to the boys and you know how she dotes on them. Though, of course, there's the thing about leaving the cottage and the money to Brian's mother,' I said. '*That* must have given them a dreadful shock. Especially David. If he's suddenly discovered that his father had a mistress and a grown up son – well!'

'I can see that,' Rosemary agreed. 'And if David was upset I expect he took it out on poor Bridget!' She put another spoonful of sugar in her coffee and stirred it vigorously. 'I wonder what really happened there – Sidney and Brian's mother – and how long it went on?'

'I should think Brian must be in his forties,' I said. 'So it must have happened a very long time ago. Perhaps when Sidney and Joan lived in London and only came down here for holidays.'

'It would have been easier for him then, really, to lead a double life. If Joan was in London he could slip down here – perhaps that's when he bought her the cottage, when the baby was born. Goodness, it's like a novel!'

'Not a very happy ending,' I said.

'Well, we don't *know* the ending yet. Perhaps we never will.'

'I might just...' I began.

'Just what?'

'I do need some more bookshelves in the study,' I said. 'I'm sure Brian would do a splendid job.'

'Brilliant!'

'Of course, he's not very chatty, normally, but – well, you never know. I'll ring him tomorrow.'

When I rang, though, I only got the answer-phone. On an impulse, I put on my coat, got the car out and drove to Withycombe. It was a frosty morning and I had to drive slowly because there were still patches of ice on the narrow road where the sun hadn't reached it between the high hedges. I wasn't sure where Rose Cottage was so I parked in the first available spot in the village and started to walk round looking for it.

I had gone all through the village and right onto the road leading to Luxborough when I finally found it. It stood a little way back from the road with a high hedge all round it. It seemed to me to have a shut-in, secretive look, but perhaps I was looking for a mystery where there was none. I opened the gate and went up the path through the garden where a few late Michaelmas daisies still bloomed. Seen close to, the cottage was very well-kept (as one would expect of Brian) and an arch of bright yellow winter jasmine round the front door lent a cheerful air.

There was no bell and I stood there hesitating for a moment, but then, assuring myself that I had a perfectly good reason for being there, I knocked on the door. There was no response. I tried again, but now the silence seemed to have a positive quality – not that there was no one there, but that someone *was* there but was deliberately not answering. I knocked again and this time I thought I heard a sound inside the house, so I called out, 'Hello! Is anyone there?'

Again, silence, then a jarring noise as if someone was dragging something across the floor.

I tried again. 'Hello. I just wanted a word with Brian. Is he there?'

Silence for a moment then a sort of panting sound, like a dog when it is tired.

'It's all right,' I said, 'if you could just give him a message.'

This time there was a response. A sort of choking, gasping scream, followed by shouting, though I could not distinguish any actual words, a horrible animal noise that made me draw back from the door and stand trembling from the shock of it. As I stood there I heard Brian's voice behind me.

'What the hell do you think you're doing? What do you want? Go away and leave us in peace.'

8

I was so shocked by the roughness and violence of his voice (so different from his usual quiet, measured tone) that I hardly heard the words. I muttered a few disconnected sentences,

'I wanted you to do a job ... just passing through the village ... so sorry...' then turned and stumbled up the path. I didn't look back as I wrenched open the gate, but I could feel he was still watching me as I almost ran down the road towards the village.

When I reached the car I sat for quite a while before I felt able to drive away. When I got home I was still badly shaken, and only when I'd had a cup of strong tea (with some brandy in it) did I feel more or less myself again.

'Whatever made you go up there anyway?' Michael asked when I told him what had happened. 'You could have left a message on his answer-phone. That's what we do.'

'You know how I hate these wretched machines,' I said. 'I never use them.'

'I know what it is. You wanted to see his mother, all that first Mrs Rochester business. Well, I hope you're satisfied!'

When he'd rung off I started to make myself some lunch. Tris was out in the garden hopefully looking for a squirrel who, attracted by the overflow from the birds' peanut feeder, had been making little darting forays into the garden in search of winter sustenance. Foss, looking for entertainment, however meagre, was sitting on the work-top watching me as I grated some cheese to make a Welsh rarebit.

'Well, Foss,' I said as I mixed the cheese with some mustard, milk and cornflour in the saucepan, '*that* was a mistake. That's the second time I've done something unkind just to satisfy my curiosity. First I upset Bridget and now goodness knows what I've done to Brian's poor mother. I think I'd better withdraw from the whole affair and let the police get on with it. That's assuming that there's anything to get on with.'

Foss showed no interest in my resolution, being occupied with batting the mustard pot across the work-top with his paw. Fortunately I caught it before it fell to the ground and shattered.

The following morning I was just taking things out of the tumble-drier, and trying to smooth out the creases with my hand so that I wouldn't have to iron them, when the door bell rang. It was Brian. For a moment I just stood there looking at him, not really knowing what to say.

'Can I have a word please, Mrs Malory?' he said. His voice was quiet and he seemed calm but rather tentative.

'Yes, of course, come in.' I led the way into the sitting room. 'Will you have a cup of tea or something?'

'No, no, thank you. I just came to apologise.'

'No really, there's no need...'

'I didn't mean to startle you like that. It's just that, well, it was my mother.'

'It's perfectly all right,' I said, 'I quite understand.'

'It's when she doesn't take her medication, you see.' He sounded agitated and spoke more quickly than usual. 'I usually see to it but I had to go out in a bit of a hurry and she promised she wouldn't forget.'

'It must be a worry for you. Look, do have that cup of tea. Come out into the kitchen with me while I make it.' I got up and he followed obediently.

I busied myself putting on the kettle and getting out the cups and milk and some biscuits to give him time to recover his composure.

He sat down at the kitchen table, not speaking for a while, then he suddenly said, 'You must be wondering about what I said, that day at his funeral.'

'I was rather surprised,' I said.

'It's a long story, but I feel I owe you an explanation.'

'Don't feel you have to tell me anything,' I said. 'I'll quite understand.'

'No, it's a relief to tell somebody. It'll be good to have it out in the open at last.'

'I gather that you have no very high opinion of Sidney Middleton?'

'That's putting it mildly. I'm sorry if he's a friend of yours, but I have to tell you what he's done to us.' He drank a little tea, as if to give himself courage to carry on. 'Way back,' he said, 'nearly fifty years ago now, when my mother was a young girl of eighteen, she met Sidney Middleton. Her father kept a livery stables and Middleton used to keep a horse there that he used to ride when he came down from London. You know he lived in London all those years, though he did come from Taviscombe and his mother still lived there.'

'Yes, I can just remember her, in that big house on West Hill.'

'My mother was a really pretty girl, she had all the lads after her, and when Middleton saw her he made a dead set at her. She was flattered, of course. He was older and had pots of money, gave her presents, took her out in his car. Her father didn't know about it. *He* said it was to be a secret and she thought that was romantic.' He gave a scornful laugh. 'It was the old story. She got pregnant. He was married and anyway wouldn't have married her even if he had been free. It was just a bit of fun to him.'

'Poor girl,' I said.

'There was no such thing as easy abortions then, of course, so she had to tell her father. My grandfather was a funny sort of man. When he was a young man he'd been a groom on a big estate and "know'd the ways of the gentlefolk" as he used to put it. So he wasn't surprised or shocked, though he was angry.'

'As well he might be!' I said.

'He got hold of Middleton and told him he had to provide for my mother and for the child otherwise he'd tell Middleton's wife and mother and there'd be a big scandal –

people weren't so free and easy about such things in those days. There was this cottage out at Withycombe. Properties like that were two a penny then so he didn't pay much for it, and it was far enough away from Taviscombe for her not to be known. My grandfather made him go to a lawyer and put it all down legal that she could live there rent free and that he'd leave it to her in his will, and there was to be some money for the child. She gave out that her husband was away with the army and she wore a wedding ring. After a bit the baby was born.'

'You?'

He shook his head. 'No, my sister.'

'Your sister? I didn't know you had a sister.'

'I don't now,' he said.

'What happened?'

'Poor little Jenny – that's what my mother called her, not that she was ever christened – she was born with something wrong with her heart, had to have an operation, but she was never right. My mother was back and forth to the hospital in Taunton, on the bus with a sick child. *He* was never there. And after a bit she died.'

'That's terrible. Couldn't your grand-parents have helped?'

'Her father died – an accident with one of the horses – and her step-mother didn't want to know. She never liked my mother, jealous, I suppose.'

He finished off the rest of his tea and sat there silently. I didn't say anything and after a while he continued.

'After a bit Middleton started coming round again and things went on like before. Then she got pregnant again and I was born. By now she'd let it out in the village that her husband had been killed overseas and she was a widow. Not that she was in the village much, just to get a few things from the shop. She kept herself to herself. Time went on and he came occasionally. He never took much notice of me – I used to be sent out when he was coming. Every time after he'd gone, she'd cry and sometimes, when I got back early I'd hear them rowing. Once, after he'd gone I saw she had bruises on her arm.' He paused for a moment at the recollection, then he went on. 'She'd lost her looks by now and one day – I can remember it like it was yesterday – he told her it was over and he'd never come again. She was practically hysterical when I got back and found her. She loved him, you see, no matter what he'd done to her.'

'How awful.'

'That's when she started to go funny – acting strange, crying all the time. She kept on phoning him. We didn't have a phone but she went down to the village to the phone box there. I can remember her coming back, soaking wet – she'd gone rushing out in the rain without a coat – sobbing her heart out. After a bit he turned nasty and said if she didn't leave him alone he'd put the police onto her.'

'He couldn't!'

'That's the sort of man he was. Then she got really bad, said there were people following her. She wouldn't go out of the house. It wasn't easy for me either, I was still at school and I had to get the food and see to the house and so on. The money still kept coming (I suppose he was still frightened of things coming out, anyway he'd signed the lawyer's paper) so we had just about enough to live on, but it was pretty hard.'

'What about the people in the village? Couldn't they help?'

'They'd all taken against her after she'd cut herself off from them. You can't really blame them. Well, she was getting worse. One day when she saw a police car passing along the lane she ran off and hid in a cupboard! That did it! I finally managed to get a doctor to see her. There was a fancy name for what she had, some sort of persecution complex, she was so frightened all the time.'

'So what happened?'

'They said she was a mental case and took her up to Tone Vale Hospital and they put me in care. After a bit they said she could come home if she took her medication, and that's how we've been ever since. When I left school I managed to get a job with a builder and after a bit I started my own business and we've been all right, financially, ever since. As soon as I was earning I never took a penny of *his* money. It's all in her bank account in case something happens to me and she needs taking care of.'

'I'm so dreadfully sorry I frightened her like that. If only I'd known...'

'Even if she'd taken her medication she probably wouldn't have opened the door. And she still won't go out, even now she knows he's dead. She's still frightened, you see.'

'Is there nothing more they can do for her?'

'If she went in for treatment they might be able to do something, but she won't. She gets upset and I won't force her to. We rub along as we are. At least...' he hesitated. 'Well, there is something. There's someone I'm very fond of. Margaret. She's divorced, her husband left her with two small children – lovely kids they are, Mark and Carol. I took Margaret home once, she's such a nice kind person I thought it might be all right, but my mother was in one of her moods and didn't speak at all and when she'd gone Mother said she'd come from the hospital to take her away again. How could I ask Margaret to come into a home like that, especially with two small children?'

'There must be some solution.'

'There is. When the old devil died he left her Rose Cottage in his will and quite a bit of money. The solicitors told me it was a lump sum he'd put aside all that time ago, to be invested, like my grandfather made him. We had the interest on it over the years, but it's increased in value by now, and like I said, there's quite a bit of money due to come to us.'

'And so I should think! Is there a problem?'

He shrugged. 'With that money, and with the money I didn't take and put away since I've been earning, there's enough to put her in a decent Home where she'll be looked after, and I'd be free. Free to marry Margaret.'

'I see.'

'But how could I do that? I'm the only one she trusts.'

'You deserve a life of your own, especially after all you've been through.'

'Yes, well.' He got up abruptly from the table. 'I've gone on long enough. But I thought you had a right to know how things are, and how they have been, and what sort of a person he really was.'

'I still can't believe it!'

'I've told you the truth.'

'Yes, I know you have. It's just such a reversal of everything. I never guessed ... he always seemed ... I'm so sorry for you both – thank you so much for telling me.'

'You're the only other person I've told apart from Margaret, but I suppose his family will have to know now because of the will. Well, it won't grieve me for people to know what he was really like.'

He moved towards the door. 'I'd better be going.'

'I would be grateful,' I said, trying to bring things back to something approaching normality again, 'if you *could* do a job for me

– I badly need some more shelves in the study. So next time you're passing...'

'I'll call in and measure up.' He seized the opportunity to change the subject gratefully.

'Right then, I'll give you a ring and let you know when I can come.'

I went back into the kitchen and began to take the remaining things out of the tumble drier. So much seemed to have happened since I'd begun this boring task that I felt could hardly take it all in. I stood for a while mechanically smoothing out a pillow case and then, pulling myself together, I folded the remaining garments and put them in the laundry basket. I really didn't feel like starting the ironing, so instead I poured myself another cup of tea (now rather cold) from the pot I'd made for Brian and, sitting down at the table, finished off the biscuits.

I was having dinner with Michael and Thea that evening and so I told them about Brian's visit.

'I know he sort of told me in confidence,' I said, 'but I thought you ought to know. I mean it clarifies things about the will and so on, and, anyway, you won't be telling anyone else.'

'I simply can't believe that Sidney could have done such things!' Thea said.

123

'I know. It's absolutely out of character for the Sidney we knew – or, *thought* we knew. But I'm really positive that everything Brian told me was the truth. You should have seen his face when he was telling me about his mother, it was heartbreaking.'

'And having to make this decision about his girlfriend. It's too cruel!'

'Would there be enough money – from the will, I mean – to keep his mother in a good nursing home?' I asked Michael.

'Oh yes, especially if he were to sell the cottage.'

'Well, I think he ought to do it,' Thea said. 'I like Brian and I think he deserves to be happy. I wonder what this Margaret is like?'

'I think I've seen her,' I said, suddenly remembering the garden centre. 'She looked nice.'

'I still can't get over Sidney,' Michael said. 'What *was* he really like? He can't have been all bad. I mean, everyone liked him.'

'We liked what he seemed to be,' I said. 'Perhaps it was all a sham. How does it go? "Whited sepulchres, which indeed appear beautiful outward, but are within full of dead men's bones".'

Thea shuddered. 'Don't!' she said. 'It's too creepy.'

124

'And what about David?' Michael said. 'What did he make of Sidney?'

'He was always chivvying his father into doing things,' I said. 'He certainly seemed to be in charge. It'll be a real surprise to *him* when he finds out about Sidney's other family! It's bound to come out because of the will. Have you spoken to him?'

'We've only communicated by letter, but he will be coming into the office sometime next week.'

'He did look awful at the funeral,' I said. 'I suppose he knew about the will then. And he hasn't asked you about the legacy and the cottage?'

'Not yet. But he is perfectly capable of putting two and two together.'

'*Can* he have known?' Thea said. 'I mean, how can you live with someone all those years and not know what they're like?'

'Lots of people do,' I said. 'You're forever reading in the papers about someone having a second family tucked away somewhere and keeping it secret for years and years.'

'Yes, I can accept that,' Thea said. 'But if Sidney behaved in such a brutal way to Brian's mother – and to him too, if you think about it – then how can he have been the sweet and gentle person we thought we knew. And did David know that?'

'And what about Joan?' I asked. 'After all, she was his wife and she was absolutely devoted to him. No, really, in spite of this business with Brian and his mother, I can't believe he was all bad.'

'Well,' Thea said, getting up, 'if you've finished your drink, would you like to come up and say goodnight to your grand-daughter before we have supper?'

As I exchanged loving greetings with the small pyjamaed figure bouncing up and down excitedly in her cot I reflected on the intense pleasures and the desperate tragedies of family life and thought, not for the first time, how lucky I am.

9

Foss must have been feeling exceptionally bored in the night because, when I went to let him out, I found he'd opened one of the drawers and hooked out most of the miscellaneous contents (rubber bands, freezer bag ties, rolls of sellotape, small fuses) and then batted a lot of them under the fridge, where he was sitting, regarding them suspiciously as if they might be trying to escape, while Tris's air of smug innocence, when I remonstrated with his feline friend, made me wonder if he, too, might have been party to the deed. I was down on my hands and knees trying to retrieve the objects with a long-handled wooden spoon, when the telephone rang. Rather creakily I got to my feet and went and answered it.

'Sheila, sorry to ring you so early.' It was Roger. 'It's just that I'll be more or less passing your door about eleven o'clock and I wondered if I might call in and have a word.'

'Yes, of course. Business or pleasure?'

'A bit of both. Sorry, I have to go now. See you then.'

I went slowly back into the kitchen. 'I wonder if it's to do with Sidney?' I said to Tris, but he was standing by the back door whining to be let out so I was left to speculate on my own.

When Roger called I had the coffee ready and a plate of home made macaroons (one of Roger's favourites) laid out in the sitting room.

'Are you wearing your policeman's hat?' I asked as I poured the coffee and pushed the sugar basin towards him.

'Sort of – though this is entirely unofficial. I must say these macaroons are good. No I just wanted to have a little chat about Sidney Middleton. I only met him briefly once or twice, but I believe you were great friends.'

'Not great friends exactly,' I said. 'My parents knew him and he's been part of my life forever, really.'

Roger took another macaroon. 'You know there's been an enquiry into his death,' he said. 'It isn't certain that it was an accident.'

'I was talking to Reg – Reg Burnaby, you know – who does all our chimneys,' I said, 'and he certainly doesn't think so. He's absolutely positive that there was nothing blocking the chimney of that stove in Sidney's kitchen.'

'So I gather. We've had our own people checking it and there certainly seemed to be no sort of obstruction, which makes it strange that he should have died of carbon monoxide poisoning.'

'Is that why the inquest was adjourned?'

'It did seem that we should make further enquiries.'

'And have you heard what Reg said about the inspection plate?' I asked.

'Yes, that's why I wanted to speak to you. I gather from him that it was you who saw the soot round the plate and told him about it.'

'And you checked it?'

'Sergeant Lister went round and had a look.'

'So?'

'From what your friend Reg says – and he's an expert in such matters – the removal of the plate would certainly explain the presence of carbon monoxide even though the chimney itself was clear.'

'And?'

'And, since it would have been possible for someone to have tampered with the plate from the outside, then we must consider if this death *was* an accident.'

'Murder?'

'Possibly.'

'Well, that's certainly what Reg thinks.'

'The only thing is,' Roger said, 'that there seems to be no possible motive for anyone to kill him. From what I've gathered Sidney Middleton was universally liked and respected, hadn't an enemy in the world.'

'Mm.' I thought for a moment, then I said, 'Actually, that may not be the case.'

'What do you mean?'

'It's beginning to look as if Sidney wasn't quite the sort of person we all thought he was.'

'In what way?'

'It seems he behaved very badly towards a couple of people – I can't give you the details because I was told in confidence. But the fact is he did some pretty awful things in the past.'

'Awful enough for someone to want to kill him?'

'Maybe. But I don't believe he – this person – would kill anyone.'

'Sheila, you do realise that, confidence or not, if this does turn out to be a murder enquiry, you must tell me what you know.'

'Yes, of course.'

Roger absently took another macaroon. 'You know it's all very peculiar. Such an odd way to kill anyone.'

'Clever, though,' I said. 'It could so easily have been taken to be an accident. I mean, if Reg hadn't had that stove to pieces so recently and swept the chimney, and if I hadn't seen that soot and Reg hadn't put two and two together...'

'Yes, well.' Roger finished his coffee and brushed a few macaroon crumbs from the front of his jacket. 'I must be getting on. Thanks for the information and for the splendid refreshments. I'll let you know how things are going and please keep me up to date on anything else you may uncover!'

As I washed up the coffee cups and emptied the percolator I was brooding about Sidney and what he was really like, and it occurred to me that there was only one thing to do. I must go and see Rosemary's mother, Mrs Dudley, who knew all about everybody, from way back, and never hesitated to speak her mind or give her opinion (however unwelcome) on any subject or any character. Since one never 'dropped in' on Mrs Dudley I needed an excuse and one came to hand almost immediately in the shape of Lorna Shepherd.

'Sheila, could you help me out?' An agitated voice on the phone. 'I'm supposed to be delivering the parish magazines and I suddenly realised I've got to go to Taunton today – something I really can't get out of – so I was wondering if you could *possibly*... Oh, that's so kind. I'll drop them off in about half an hour, if that's all right.'

Before I went out to deliver the magazines I telephoned Mrs Dudley. As I had hoped, I got Elsie, still referred to by Mrs Dudley as 'my maid' and by everyone else as 'her slave'.

'Elsie,' I said, 'I'm delivering the parish magazines this afternoon and I wondered if Mrs Dudley would be up to having a little chat when I bring hers.'

Elsie came back to the phone with her instructions. 'Mrs Dudley says she'll be having her rest after lunch but she'll be pleased to see you at four o'clock for tea.'

It was nearly five past four (delivering parish magazines usually means a great deal of chat on the doorstep) when I arrived and, as I entered the sitting room, Mrs Dudley glanced pointedly at the clock but didn't comment on my lateness.

'Do come in Sheila, and sit by the fire, the weather is very seasonable.'

In addition to the central heating there was

a log fire burning in the grate ('I do like to see a proper fire'), but, fortunately I knew of old how overheated the room would be so I'd dressed accordingly. Mrs Dudley, elegant as always and with her hair carefully arranged, stretched out a thin hand and waved me to a chair beside her. She was getting rather deaf now, but refused to admit it ('Absolute nonsense. I can hear perfectly well when people don't *mumble* – in my day we were taught to speak properly') so she now preferred one to one conversations with her interlocutor close at hand.

'It's very good to see you,' she said. 'I know how busy all you young people are. I hardly ever see or hear from Rosemary these days, she's always busy, off on some ploy or other.'

This was a black lie since I knew for a fact that Rosemary visited her mother frequently and spoke to her on the telephone every single day. Mrs Dudley was perfectly aware that I knew this, but we both politely ignored the fact in the interest of promoting Mrs Dudley's view of herself, something that we had been doing for as long as I could remember.

I put the parish magazine down on the little side table beside her.

'Why are you delivering the magazines?' she asked sharply. 'Lorna Shepherd always does that, and they're usually several days late. So inefficient.'

'She had to go to Taunton today.'

'Oh really. What for?'

'I don't know.'

Mrs Dudley was obviously disappointed in me as a source of information but she said graciously, 'Well, it's good to see you. We can have tea now.'

She rang the small handbell at her side and Elsie wheeled in the tea-trolley. In addition to the usual array of cakes (all made by Elsie, of course) there was a plate of tiny triangular tomato sandwiches that I knew from experience would not be flaccid and soggy as my tomato sandwiches always are, but of a perfect texture, the bread, butter and tomato all combining in the kind of perfection that only a real culinary artist can achieve. After I had poured the tea from the heavy silver tea pot and passed various plates of comestibles to Mrs Dudley, who, I was glad to see, still retained her excellent appetite, she said, 'Do sit down Sheila – it's most unrestful to see you bobbing up and down like that!'

She took another sandwich and launched

into a detailed description of her latest battle with her doctor which I listened to on autopilot, as it were (since it was an old battle re-fought many times over) while I enjoyed my delicious tea. I was jerked into attention however when I heard her say, '...and, of course, it was Dr Macdonald who was called to Sidney Middleton, though naturally it was too late for him to do anything *there*.'

'That was very sad,' I said.

'A very *peculiar* way to go,' Mrs Dudley said disapprovingly. 'Those old stoves are very unreliable. I always say it's false economy not to replace things when they are worn out.'

'I believe the stove was perfectly all right. Reg Burnaby serviced it quite recently and swept the chimney.'

'Oh well, if Reg said so it must have been.' Reg was one of Mrs Dudley's retinue of 'little men' who did things for her and so could do no wrong. 'In that case I really don't see how it could have happened.'

I told her about the inspection plate and what Reg had said.

'You mean it wasn't an accident? That he was killed deliberately?' she asked quickly.

'It seems possible.'

'Well, I'm not surprised,' she said. 'Sheila

dear, will you very kindly cut me a small piece of coffee cake – I said small, dear, not *minute*. Thank you.'

'But everyone was so fond of Sidney,' I said. 'He was very popular.'

Mrs Dudley considered this remark while cutting her fair sized piece of cake into small portions. 'Oh no, Sheila, not what I would call popular. I never liked the man myself.'

To those of us who knew her, this meant that, at some point, the person 'not liked' had disagreed with her about something, many years ago perhaps, but Mrs Dudley rarely forgave what she took to be a slight and certainly never forgot one. There was quite a list of people who had been cast into the outer darkness in this way, but I hadn't known that Sidney Middleton had been on it.

'Really?'

'Oh no. He may have charmed a lot of people but I saw him for what he really was.'

'And what was that?' I asked.

'Oh, selfish. Selfish to the core.'

'But he always seemed to me to be doing what David wanted. We always thought *he* was the selfish one.'

Mrs Dudley gave what in anyone else would have been a snort. 'Nonsense,' she said. 'That is what he wanted everyone to believe, but he never really did anything he didn't want to do. And as for that poor wife of his...'

'Oh, surely! They were devoted!'

'She was devoted to him, certainly.'

'But they were childhood sweethearts,' I said.

'They wouldn't have been if her father hadn't been one of the richest men in Taviscombe.'

'You mean he married her for her money?'

'And stayed married to her because her father had the sense to tie the money up in a Trust so that he couldn't get at the capital.'

'Good heavens!'

'All that business about Ruby Weddings, a party and all that silly fuss – absolutely ridiculous! *She* would never admit that anything was wrong, of course, but then she was a poor little creature, no idea of standing up for herself. But he always had a roving eye, not, I am sure, that she would ever bring herself to believe it.'

'I never had any idea!'

'Oh, they kept up a facade, right enough, but *I* knew the sort of thing that was going on.'

'Really?'

'Little Mavis Freeman – do you remember her? Her mother used to do some dressmaking for me – *she* had her head turned by him. This was years ago. Poor Mrs Freeman came to me in great distress, because she couldn't get Mavis to see sense. She was afraid the girl might get pregnant and then what would become of her? Of course that was when he'd moved away from Taviscombe and was living in London. Goodness knows what he got up to there!' Mrs Dudley always had the gravest doubts about what went on in London since it was outside her jurisdiction. 'He used to come down quite often – he *said* to see his mother – a thoroughly disagreeable woman, very high opinion of herself, lived in that house on West Hill with the monkey puzzle tree in the garden. But I've no doubt he was down here for *quite* another reason. And Mavis Freeman wasn't the only one, not by a long chalk.'

I shook my head in bewilderment. 'I just can't imagine how we could all have been so wrong about him,' I said.

Mrs Dudley gave a grim little smile. 'Men,' she said, 'if they've got that sort of superficial charm, they can get away with anything.' Mrs Dudley had an even lower opinion of men than she had of women. There were a favoured few, like my husband Peter and (probably because of him) Michael, but they were the rare exceptions. Her husband, Rosemary's father, was in a different category, since she had chosen to marry him and that automatically gave him the status of a consort. Besides, he had died tragically in a motor accident when Rosemary was quite young.

'I suppose so. But,' I said, 'what about David? Surely he must have known what his father was like.'

'They sent him away to school when he was seven and then he was at University, and I've no doubt his father kept up appearances when he was at home.'

'But now,' I persisted, 'these last years, since his mother died, he seems to have taken over his father's life. He's always trying to make Sidney do things he doesn't want to do, like going into a Home.'

'Yes, but,' asked Mrs Dudley triumphantly, 'when has he ever got his way? When has he ever made his father do anything he didn't want to do?'

I considered this. 'Yes – I see what you mean. You think it was all an act on Sidney's part?'

'Exactly.'

'And he allowed everyone to think that David was bullying him?'

'Certainly. Sidney Middleton was a thoroughly unpleasant man, I am delighted to think that I refused him.'

'*What!*'

'Many years ago, when I was just eighteen, he proposed to me.'

'Good heavens!'

'There was no question of my accepting him. Even then I could see what sort of person he was. He took it quite badly and went around making very unpleasant remarks about me, which was typical. He was *not* a gentleman. So he married Joan Wishart for her money and then the war came and he went away.'

'I'd no idea – Rosemary never said...'

'I have never found it necessary to tell her.'

'But...'

'And,' Mrs Dudley said, giving me a severe glance, 'I would prefer you not to mention it to her.'

10

I'd arranged to go to an art exhibition with Rosemary the next day, which left me very little time to decide whether or not I should tell her about Sidney's proposal to her mother. If Mrs Dudley gave you instructions you always obeyed them. The thought of what she'd say if she found out you *hadn't* was too terrible to contemplate. She had specifically told me not to tell Rosemary and my immediate instinct was dutiful submission to her command – for command it was, however mildly expressed. But then, Rosemary was my friend, my oldest, dearest friend, so how could I not tell her? All right, it wasn't an earth-shattering, life-changing piece of information that Mrs Dudley had dropped so casually into the conversation, but it was inconceivable that I should know something about Rosemary's mother that she didn't. If I didn't tell her I'd feel uncomfortable for the rest of my life.

'I thought,' Rosemary said when she came to collect me, 'I'd give Roger a picture for

Christmas. I never know what to get him, and Jilly's no help. He likes Victorian watercolours and most of the paintings at these exhibitions are mostly traditional. Anyway, even if there's nothing there, it's at Halseway Manor and I've always wanted to see what it's like inside, and we can get lunch there so it'll be a day out.'

'Yes,' I said absently, 'lovely.'

Rosemary looked at me quizzically. 'What's the matter? You haven't heard a word I said.'

'Actually,' I said, 'actually, there's something I need to tell you.' And I told her about my conversation with Mrs Dudley. 'For goodness sake,' I concluded, 'don't ever let her know that I told you. She'd never forgive me, and I don't think I could survive not being forgiven by your mother!'

'Oh, that!' Rosemary said. 'I know all about *that*. Aunt Amy told me about it years ago. She thought it was a tremendous joke.'

'Oh, really,' I said crossly. 'All that agonising for nothing!'

Rosemary laughed. 'Poor you!' she said. 'No, I think Aunt Amy was a bit put out that he didn't propose to *her* – he was quite a catch in those days. But if Sidney was beastly about her afterwards, it does explain why Mother's never had a good word to say about him ever since.'

The bright winter sun had melted the early morning frost and it was a beautiful day.

'I could really do with a day out,' Rosemary said. 'I've had to do all Mother's Christmas shopping as well as my own and Jack's, not to mention the Christmas cards. Well, Jack does some of his – mostly business acquaintances abroad, but he always leaves them till the last minute and I have to queue for ages at the post office and spend a fortune sending them airmail.' She braked sharply to avoid a low-flying bird. 'I wish they wouldn't *do* that! And I lost last year's Christmas card list and we keep getting cards from people I've forgotten.'

There were quite a few people at the exhibition when we got there, many, perhaps, like Rosemary in search of that elusive Christmas present. The pictures were of a high quality. Painting is a popular pastime among the many retired people in the district and the beauty of the surrounding countryside tempts even the less gifted to try to capture it. The difficulty for an amateur of taking a likeness meant that there were few portraits, but the still life was popular – jugs, fruit and more homely domestic objects – and many people had chosen flower painting, the solitary iris or the bunch of primroses and snowdrops being most in evidence.

'There are quite a few that he *might* like,' Rosemary said. 'What do you think?'

'Some of the landscapes are charming,' I said. 'That one of a cottage by the stream is really quite Victorian – a bit sentimental and bland, though.'

'Mm, yes. Oh, I do think I might get that one, over there for Delia – the one of a group of ponies on Winsford Hill. Did I tell you she's into horses now, I'm afraid? A couple of her friends have their own ponies, so of course she's agitating for one too. I know Jilly doesn't want her to get into the whole Pony Club thing – dreadfully expensive!'

'Better not get the picture then,' I said, 'if it's going to encourage her.'

'I suppose not. Anyway, I'm giving her some money for clothes and record vouchers and things. Jilly said for heaven's sake don't *choose* anything for her. You are lucky, you can still buy things for Alice. Make the most of it while you can.'

We moved slowly round the two rooms

devoted to the exhibition and I stopped before one of them. 'Oh yes,' I said. 'That's the one.'

It was quite a small picture, mostly in greys and browns, a sweeping view of the moor in winter, with a line of beech trees (a beech hedge grown up into trees over the years) on the horizon. You could almost feel the hardness of the ground, the brittleness of the wind-scorched heather, and see the movement of the clouds across the sky – it was the very essence of that place at that time.

'It is, isn't it.' Rosemary went up and peered at it closely. 'I wonder who did it? Someone called David Middleton. Good heavens, not *David Middleton* – it can't be!'

'I suppose it might be someone with the same name,' I suggested.

'Well, whoever it is,' Rosemary said 'I'm going to buy it now, before anyone else does.'

We went over to the table where a middle-aged lady of vaguely artistic appearance was handing out typed lists of the pictures.

'I'd like to buy that landscape by David Middleton,' Rosemary said. 'Number – what is it? – number thirty-two.'

'Ah yes, number thirty-two.' She looked

145

down the list and named a very modest sum. 'Such a gifted man, I believe he is an accountant. I suppose,' she added with a slight smile, 'painting is a pleasant relaxation from such a demanding profession. I'll put a sold label on it and perhaps you would collect it at the end of the week after the exhibition is over.'

Sitting in the converted stables, now a lunch room, we continued to speculate on the identity of the artist.

'There can't be two local accountants called David Middleton,' Rosemary said firmly. 'Jack would have mentioned it.' Rosemary's husband Jack is also an accountant.

'But to have painted that picture,' I said. 'Such sensitivity. And to have chosen to paint the moor in winter – most people go for the heather in bloom and all that sort of thing – whoever did it must have a really selective eye.'

'I must admit,' Rosemary said, picking the pieces of red pepper out of her salad, 'David Middleton wouldn't be the first person I'd associate with anything artistic, let alone a picture like that.'

'Exactly. It really is quite extraordinary. Perhaps we've been misjudging him all these years.'

'Mind you,' Rosemary said, 'just because someone paints a good picture doesn't mean he's a good person.'

'No,' I agreed, 'not *good* exactly, but, as I said, there's sensitivity there and that isn't something you'd think of in connection with David.'

'You mean the way he treated his father? So dreadfully bossy, and poor little Bridget, too.'

'Perhaps we were wrong about that,' I said. 'Perhaps we were wrong about all the Middletons.'

'What do you mean?' Rosemary asked.

'Oh, I don't know,' I replied, wanting to change the subject. 'Shall we have some of that carrot cake? It looks quite nice and moist.'

I was hovering round the vegetable section of the supermarket wondering whether it was worthwhile buying a punnet of strawberries or if they'd be as tasteless as out of season fruit always is, when someone greeted me.

'Sheila, it's been such a long time since I saw you, how are you getting on?'

I turned round and saw that it was Betty Goddard. I was quite shocked to see her.

For once she was looking her age, thinner and really old.

'How are *you?*' I asked. 'You don't look at all well – have you had this wretched flu that's been going round?'

'No, I haven't, but Bill hasn't been at all well. He's had a nasty go of bronchitis, hasn't been able to shake it off. And then there was this other thing–' She broke off as if she'd said too much.

'I'm so sorry to hear about Bill,' I said. 'Do you think he'd like a visit?'

She brightened. 'Oh yes, Sheila, it would really cheer him up to see a fresh face. He's been stuck indoors for weeks now and you know what a one he's always been for getting out and about.'

'*Not* the easiest of patients?'

She laughed. 'Well, you know what men are like! But he'd really like to see you, I know.'

'Would tomorrow do? About elevenish?'

'That would be lovely Well, I must get on, he'll be waiting for his lunch. I think I'll try and get him a nice piece of smoked haddock – he's got very difficult over his food, it might tempt him to eat a bit. I'll see you tomorrow then, Sheila. That will be nice.'

I rejected the strawberries in favour of a

not very ripe mango and went on my way.

Bill and Betty lived in a very nice bungalow on the outskirts of Taviscombe, high up with a view down over the town to the sea. They'd had a small conservatory built on at the back and it was here that I found Bill sitting with a rug over his knees, though the heating had been turned up, reading the local paper. His face lit up when Betty ushered me in.

'Sheila! It was good of you to come. I get so sick of sitting looking at the same four walls all the time.'

'Oh,' I protested, 'you've got a lovely view from here.'

'Yes, well, you can get fed up with anything after a bit.'

Betty brought in two cups of coffee and said 'I'll leave you two to chat while I get on with my ironing' then went away.

'So,' I said, 'how are you? Betty said you'd been poorly.'

'Just my old bronchitis again. Worse, this time. I suppose it gets worse when you're old, everything wearing out.'

'Come on, now, you're strong as an ox. Once the nice weather comes you'll be fine. How long have you had the bronchitis? We missed you at Sidney Middleton's funeral, were you bad then?'

Bill started to speak but was seized by a fit of coughing and had to drink a little coffee before he could continue.

'No,' he said grimly, 'that was before I had my attack. Something happened...' He began to cough again.

'Have some more coffee,' I said. 'Don't try to talk for a bit.'

He finished the rest of the coffee and was silent for a moment, as if recovering himself.

'There's something I want to tell you,' he said at last.

'Look, if it's upsetting you...'

'No, it's something you ought to know. Something everyone should know.'

His tone, so unlike the Bill Goddard I'd always known, worried me.

'Are you sure you're all right?' I asked. 'Shall I call Betty?'

'No,' he said impatiently. 'I'm all right. I just want to tell you.'

'Go on, then,' I said, seeing that nothing else would satisfy him.

'Well, you know how I had to clear out our Vera's stuff when she died and how I found these letters she'd never opened after Frank was killed? Well, I read them.' He paused for a minute then went on, 'There were a couple from Frank, the usual stuff we all wrote home – everything's OK, not to worry, soon be back, can't wait to see you, that kind of thing – and there was one from his friend Ted. I'd like you to read it.'

He pushed the newspaper to one side and handed me a couple of sheets of paper. They had been torn out of a notebook and the writing in pencil was hard to read.

'Take it over to the light,' Bill said. 'You'll see better there.'

I got up, went over to the end of the conservatory and began to read. The letter was dated 20th February 1945.

Dear Vera

I am writing to you from the field hospital here somewhere in Belgium. Waiting my turn on the operating table. I expect Frank will have told you about me because we've been mates together right through. We always got on a treat and hoped we'd see it through together but it was not to be. Frank was my mate and he ought not to have died like he did. After four years in the army I know nobody high-up is going to believe me or do anything about it, but I owe it to Frank to make sure you know the truth.

At the beginning of this month we'd just crossed the River Maas and was moving through these pine forests to a place called Geldern. Mr Middleton's section was up front when he got orders to do a recce on a farmhouse they said was in a clearing half a mile ahead. There was a bridge near the house and they wanted to know if it had been blown up. Mr Middleton was detailed to go forward with one man to find out if Jerry was in the house. The rest of the section was left in charge of Frank and was to wait until Mr Middleton and me got back with the all clear.

Mr Middleton and me got to the edge of the wood and there was the house a couple of hundred yards away in the middle of this snow-covered field. We had a good look through Mr Middleton's glasses and couldn't see no sign of life. Mr Middleton says, Looks like Jerry's pulled out. I think we've seen all we need. Well, I says, if it's their paratroopers over there, they'll know what they're about. They'll be holed up so you could walk right up to them without seeing them. Don't you think we'd better try and get a bit closer in?

Are you crazy, he says. How far do you think we'd get? There's no cover in any direction and they'd spot us against the snow before we'd gone ten paces. So we went back to the section and Mr Middleton gave the order to advance and the boys moved out of that field not expecting *any trouble.*

Jerry let us get about half-way to the house before he opened up with his Spandaus. We didn't stand a chance. Your Frank bled to death, I reckon. I saw him trying to get his field dressing out, but I couldn't get to him. The funny part was that Jerry must have pulled out soon after. They were too smart to hang around once they'd given away their position. And no sooner had they gone than Mr Middleton jumped up from somewhere and bolted back across the field and into the wood. Never stopped to see what had happened to the rest of us. Not a scratch on him. I don't know how long it was before the Company came forward and picked us up. By the time they come up I was the only man left alive. Those who weren't killed outright bled to death in the snow like your poor Frank.

Mr Middleton will live to come home and play the big hero and it's not right. I hope the news will not cause you too much pain, but I thought you ought to know. I'll put this in an envelope with your name and address on it and one of the nurses has promised to send it on if I don't pull through and can do it myself. I thought you ought to know.

Yours faithfully

Ted Barker

The last few paragraphs were difficult to read, the writing was fainter and the lines straggled crookedly across the paper.

'There was a note on the envelope,' Bill said, 'saying that Ted died of his wounds.'

I handed him back the paper. 'I didn't know Sidney Middleton was with Frank in the war.'

'Yes, he used to speak about Frank, say what a fine chap he was.' Bill's voice was expressionless, then he burst out, 'We all looked up to him, thought he was marvellous. No side for an officer, we used to say, on Christian name terms we were, a real gentleman, he often used to come and have a drink with the lads in the Legion – and all the time...'

'That's horrible!'

'He thought he was safe, you see. Everyone else was dead – even poor Ted Barker – so there was no one to say what had happened, no one knew it was his fault. His fault because he was a sodding coward – sorry, Sheila – because he never did a proper recce. All those men dead and he saved his own skin.'

'It's unbelievable.'

'It's *true*. Someone everybody looked up

to, everybody said how wonderful he was –
felt sorry for him having to go into a Home
– and all the time...'

'Bill, I'm so sorry It must have been the
most awful shock.'

'It was that all right. When I read that
letter I thought nothing else would ever
make me feel so bad. But there was
something else.' He stopped abruptly and I
looked at him enquiringly. 'Oh yes,' he went
on, 'something that made me feel even
worse than Ted's letter. There was a letter
from Frank's commanding officer saying
what a wonderful person he was and how he
died bravely in battle, how his death was
instantaneous and he didn't suffer.' Bill's
face was twisted with pain as he made the
effort to continue. 'All the things that
commanding officers write to the wives and
mothers. A lovely letter you might say, a real
comfort. Except – except that Frank's
commanding officer, the man who wrote
the letter was Sidney Middleton, the man
responsible for getting him killed.'

11

I went back slowly and sat down again, opposite Bill. 'I don't know what to say. It's all so awful.'

He nodded. 'There's times I can't really believe it,' he said. 'Times I can't believe anyone could be such a – such a hypocrite. How could he live with himself after that? And to keep quiet all these years. Everyone thought so highly of him. More fools us!'

'Not quite everyone,' I said, and I told him about Brian and his mother. I didn't mention their names, of course, but simply told him their story.

'Even then, even before the war – what sort of man *was* he!'

'A pretty rotten one, obviously,' I said, 'and we might never have found out...When did you read the letter, was it before he died?'

'Yes, it was. When I read it I was all for going round there and having it out with him but Betty stopped me, said wait till I'd calmed down a bit. I wish I had now – I wish

I'd been able to tell him *somebody* knew what sort of person he really was. Well, I can't do that now, but I can tell everyone else, let them know what he did. I'd have done it before, only this bronchitis kept me indoors. But as soon as I'm better I'm going down to the Legion and I'm going to tell Ernie and Fred and those of us who're left, who remember him.'

'It'll be a shock to them,' I said.

'It certainly will,' Bill agreed grimly. 'There'll be some hard things said when this gets out.'

I thought about David. Had he known any of these terrible things about his father?

'What about David,' I asked Bill. 'What are you going to do about telling him?'

Bill shrugged. 'I don't know,' he said. 'Seems to me he ought to know. I never liked the lad, thought he bullied his father – well, perhaps we got that wrong too.'

I thought of the painting. 'Perhaps we did.'

On my way out I had a word with Betty as she came out of the kitchen. 'I was sorry to see Bill looking not himself,' I said. 'But I can quite see that this thing has upset him very much.'

'He wanted to tell you,' Betty said, wiping her hands on her apron. 'He thought you ought to know seeing as you were a friend of that man. I hope it didn't upset you too much.'

'It was upsetting,' I agreed, 'but I've been hearing a few things about Sidney in the last few weeks that have really surprised me. Poor Bill. It must have been such a dreadful shock, learning about it like that!'

'I've been really worried about him,' Betty said, drawing me into the sitting room and lowering her voice. 'He came home from Vera's that day and just handed me the letter to read. Well, you can imagine how I felt, not just about the letter but seeing him like that. He'd worked himself up into a terrible state, wanted to go round to Sidney Middleton's straight away, calling him all sorts! It was awful, I was really afraid of what he might do.'

'It must have been.'

'I managed to get him calmed down a bit, but he didn't sleep a wink that night – nor did I, for that matter – and the next day he went out for a long walk, didn't say where he was going, just that he needed to clear his head. He went out several days after that, one day he didn't get back till after dark. I was really worried about him by then, I can tell you.'

'Poor Betty, what did you do?'

'It had got to such a state I was going to get the doctor to him, I thought he was having a breakdown or something. But then he got this chill. The weather was quite bad some of the days he was out and that turned to bronchitis – he's always had this chest – so I got Dr Macdonald in to see him anyway and he put him on antibiotics and he's gradually getting better.'

'Did you tell Dr Macdonald anything...?'

'No, Bill had to stay in the house, being ill and everything, and he was gradually getting to be a bit more his old self, so I thought I'd leave it for now. But I am glad he told you, when I said you were coming he said he'd tell you. He needed to tell someone.'

As I was leaving the bungalow I met Myra Norton coming up the road. As usual she was full of chat.

'Hello, have you been to see Mr and Mrs Goddard? Poor souls. He's been quite seedy. They had to have the doctor in, it might easily have turned to pneumonia at his age. I went and got the prescription for him. Well, poor Mrs Goddard didn't like to leave him and what are neighbours for? Still, this weather isn't very kind to old people, is it? I was saying to Jim the other day, just you wrap up warm, you don't want to get a bad chest like poor Mr Goddard.'

'I think he's making a good recovery,' I said.

'That's nice. Oh well, once we get Christmas over it'll soon be Spring and then we'll all feel much better!'

As I went on my way I thought that even the promised Spring wouldn't do much to make Bill Goddard feel better, nor Betty for that matter. This further discovery of Sidney Middleton's appalling behaviour, emphasising just how wrong we had all been about him, depressed me dreadfully.

'"There's no art to find the mind's construction in the face",' I said to Thea when I told her what had happened. 'How does it go on? "He was a gentleman on whom I built an absolute trust". That certainly applies to Sidney!'

'We all did,' she said. 'After all we had no reason to think otherwise. He had a lot of charm, he was always so sympathetic, such a good listener, that's how he deceived us.'

'I suppose we just took him at his face value. But that's what you do with people, isn't it? Unless you have a reason to think otherwise, and we had no reason.'

'If Bill Goddard tells people about the

letter then soon everyone will know how awful Sidney was,' Thea said thoughtfully. 'What will that do to David, I wonder?'

'He certainly looked peculiar at the funeral,' I said, 'and Bridget even more so. Perhaps they'd found out something about Sidney by then.'

'Well they'd certainly have heard about the will and Brian's mother. That must have shaken them. It's all so extraordinary. What *I* think is...'

We were interrupted by Alice, newly awoken from her afternoon rest in the neighbouring room, who appeared clutching her comfort blanket and demanding a drink of milk and our undivided attention. So I never did get to hear Thea's theory.

I did, however, see Bridget a few days later. Just for a change I took Tris up onto the hill for his afternoon walk. There is a sort of plateau half-way up the hill, surrounded by woodland and sheltered from the wind, but with good paths and a nice view of the sea down below. It is very popular with dog walkers and, as usual, there were several cars parked on the bit of hard standing. On this particular day, though, the wind, coming in from the sea, made it less than pleasant. I got out of the car reluctantly and even Tris, usually eager to be out and about, had to be lifted from the back seat and set on the path, where he cowered a little as the wind blew his ears back. Still, his natural enthusiasm to investigate the delicious smells all around soon had him straining at his lead and pulling me along. I steered him towards the trees out of the worst of the wind and we ambled along on the path, our feet sinking into the soft covering of pine needles. I inhaled appreciatively the woody smell of the conifers and began to enjoy the walk. In the distance I saw another dog walker who had braved the brisk weather and as we approached I saw that it was Bridget with her spaniel. She didn't see me immediately, but when she did see me and appeared to recognise me, to my surprise, she veered off sharply and took another path that ran off at an angle round the side of the hill, and by the time I had reached it she was out of sight. It was perfectly obvious that, for some reason or another, she had wanted to avoid me. I wondered if it was just me she wanted to avoid, or just anyone who knew her. I also wondered why.

When I got back to where the cars were parked there was no sign of her. Apparently she'd already made her escape. I sat for a while in the car thinking about what had happened. Bridget had never been what you might call a forthcoming person, but usually she was prepared to chat about things in general when we met. Obviously something had occurred that she didn't want to talk about – or something that David had told her not to talk about – and it had to be about Sidney. I wondered how long it would be before the gossip started.

'What's all this about Sidney Middleton, then?' Anthea demanded as we were sorting out the toys donated to the local children's home for Christmas. It was cold in Brunswick Lodge because there was something wrong with the heating and I was concentrating on trying to keep my hands warm while sorting through a box of picture books.

'What do you mean?' I asked.

'I saw Mrs Pudsey at the Red Cross coffee morning yesterday and she said there was some sort of scandal about him. She said Fred was full of it.'

'Really?'

'Apparently Fred went to see Bill Goddard – he's had bronchitis and can't get out – and he told him the whole story.

Something to do with the war, somewhere abroad I think, I didn't get the details. Mrs Pudsey was a bit vague about what actually happened, but it seems that Sidney behaved very badly and people were killed. It all sounded most peculiar. Do you know anything about it?'

'I had heard something, but I don't really know,' I said mendaciously. Somehow I couldn't quite bring myself to be the one to bring the truth out into the open. Ridiculous, really, since Sidney had been a vile person who certainly didn't deserve any sort of consideration. He fully deserved to have his memory blackened, it was just that I didn't want to be the one who actually did it.

'Oh.' Anthea was clearly disappointed in me. 'I thought that since you knew him so well you might know what it was all about.'

'It seems that we none of us knew him,' I said.

'That's nonsense,' Anthea said firmly. 'People can't hide what they are. I'd trust my judgement any day. Anyway, think of what he did for this place. Brunswick Lodge owes him a great deal. Not only the money he gave – and he always gave very generously to any appeal – but think of all the garden parties we had at Lamb's Cottage every summer, they raised a lot of money.'

'Giving money and things like that doesn't necessarily make you a good person,' I said. 'Especially if you're as well off as Sidney was. He must have made an absolute fortune in the City, so it wouldn't mean all that much to him.'

'Sorry to interrupt you, but I'm going to have to switch off the electricity.' Jim Norton had come in while we were talking. 'Can you manage without for about half an hour?'

'Yes, of course,' I said, ignoring Anthea's immediate protest. 'We don't really need the light on – it's quite light enough for us to see what we're doing.'

'I suppose so,' Anthea said grudgingly. 'We'll just have to wait for our cup of coffee.'

'I'll make one for all of us when you've finished,' I said, with what I hoped was a conciliatory smile. 'It's really good of you to be doing all this. I don't know how we'd have managed without you!'

Jim Norton went away and we got on with what we had been doing.

'Oh dear, a jigsaw puzzle,' Anthea said, holding it up. 'A big one of Tower Bridge. That will never do!'

'Won't it?' I enquired, wondering what it was about one of our most popular landmarks that made it unsuitable for children.

'Secondhand jigsaws are never a good idea,' Anthea said. 'There's *always* a piece missing and you can imagine what problems that causes.'

'Yes, of course. Oh look, isn't he sweet?' I exclaimed, fishing out a woolly lamb from one of the boxes. 'Such a lovely expression.'

Anthea gave a non-committal smile but the lamb appeared to send her mind back to our earlier conversation.

'I wonder what will happen to Lamb's Cottage?' she said. 'I suppose David won't live there. Such a shame, that garden was ideal for open air functions.' She straightened up and lifted her empty box off the trestle table and put it on the floor. 'It must be worth a pretty penny,' she said thoughtfully, 'with house prices as they are and it stands right back from the road. Oh well, I suppose someone will buy it as a second home. It really is a disgrace.'

She was off on one of her favourite subjects and, although I made suitable noises of agreement as required I abstracted my mind and thought about the effect a full revelation of Sidney's misdeeds would have.

Not that anyone else would know about Brian and his mother, except David, oh and Michael, Thea and me, but we'd never say anything. I wondered if David had told Bridget, if she knew what sort of person her father-in-law had been. It was strange, now I came to think of it, that Bridget had apparently seen so little of him. The more I thought about it the stranger the whole Middleton set-up seemed.

'So what do you *think?*' Anthea said impatiently. It was obviously not the first time she'd asked the question, whatever it was. 'Should we include computer games or not? Do *concentrate*, Sheila, or we'll never get done.'

'Oh yes, I think so,' I said, snatching a thought out of the air. 'I believe they've got several computers at St Mary's.'

'Oh well, if you say so,' Anthea said grudgingly.

The lights came on suddenly and Jim Norton appeared. 'All done,' he said. 'It should be all right now.'

'Oh marvellous,' I said. 'I'll go and make us that coffee.'

I saw Bridget in the post office when I called in there on my way home, but I deliberately turned away as I stood in the queue so that she didn't notice me as she went past. I didn't want her to have to pretend she hadn't seen me, which would have been embarrassing for us both. Still, I was curious to know why she was avoiding me.

I thought about it all as I drove home. Thanks to Reg, the police now knew that Sidney's death was not an accident. Obviously someone had removed the inspection plate on the chimney in order to kill him. The fact that somebody had hated Sidney enough to murder him, which seemed so unlikely at the time, now seemed very possible. Both Brian and Bill had reason enough to hate him, though I found it very difficult to think of Bill as a murderer. Brian, on the other hand, had a double motive – his mother's condition and his own unhappy childhood and now this chance of happiness that seemed to be denied him. As a handyman he would probably have been familiar with flues and chimneys and would have known how to sabotage them.

But then, Bill had been out, after dark too, just about the time of the murder, and, although he was an old man and a bit frail now, it wouldn't have taken much strength to unscrew that plate. I still found it almost impossible to imagine Bill, however horrific the circumstances, actually murdering someone. But Bill had been a soldier too and seen action in France. Presumably he'd killed people then. Perhaps if he'd thought of it as a sort of extension of a war situation, then perhaps he just *might* have been in the frame of mind to avenge his brother's death – and, indeed, the death of all those other soldiers (Frank's mates) in the section.

It was such a simple way to kill someone. As Anthea said, Lamb's Cottage stood well back from the road, there were quite a lot of shrubs to provide cover for an intruder, and, besides, not many people went down that lane, especially after dark. All the murderer had to do was to unscrew the plate when he knew the stove was lit – most of the time in the Winter – leave the chimney to do its work and then come back early next morning and replace it before anyone was about. The fact that Sidney hadn't been found straight away had helped, of course, but he was an old man and it wasn't very likely that he would have survived a whole evening of carbon monoxide poisoning. He'd just have lost consciousness and that would have been that. As Mrs Harrison said, he'd just slipped away. Not a bad way to go, really. Better than he deserved, some people might say.

I put the car away, went in and fed the animals, still turning over in my mind the whole extraordinary business. I wondered if Roger would hear the gossip about Sidney – what Bill had to say would soon be common knowledge. And what about Brian's story? Something told to me in confidence. But should Roger know? They were both motives for Sidney's murder, so should I tell him? My instinct was to keep quiet. I was very fond of Bill and deeply sorry for Brian. After all, I had no evidence that either of them was actually involved.

It would be unkind to expose them to suspicion and questioning just because...

My mind went round and round until with a conscious effort I put it all to one side and concentrated on getting supper. To cheer myself up I thought I'd make a special fruit salad. The unripe mango I'd bought that day I'd seen Betty in the supermarket should be just about ready by now. But when I picked it out of the fruit bowl I found it was over-ripe, mouldy down one side and had to be thrown away.

12

'Sheila,' Rosemary said, when I went round there the next day to take a pot of hyacinths I'd planted for her, 'what's all this about Sidney and Bill Goddard? Anthea was going on about it and I couldn't make head or tail of what she was getting at.'

I told her Bill's story and then, because Rosemary is my oldest and dearest friend and I always tell her everything, I told her about Brian and his mother too.

'Brian told me that in confidence,' I said, 'so don't tell anyone else. Well, I suppose it would be all right if you mentioned it to Jack.'

'He wouldn't say a word. But Sheila, what an extraordinary thing – we thought Sidney was such a nice person. How *could* we have been taken in like that!'

'I know. I can still hardly believe it. But there you are. I don't know which is the most awful, that horrible thing in the war or all those years of misery for Brian and his mother.'

'That woman we saw him with at the garden centre, I suppose she's the one he wants to marry.'

'I think so. She looked nice. I wonder if Brian's heard Bill's story yet.'

'I wouldn't be surprised,' Rosemary said. 'Word gets about pretty quickly, especially if it's something to someone's discredit. I wonder what he'll make of it?'

'I should think he'll be jolly glad Sidney's real nature is being exposed at last.'

'Nasty for David and Bridget.'

I told her about Bridget avoiding me up on the hill. 'It's almost as if she can't face me.'

'That's not surprising,' Rosemary declared. 'Would you!'

'No, I suppose not. Still it's a bit unfair on her, poor little thing.'

'She's always struck me as being a feeble sort of person, but then you'd have to be to be married to someone like David.'

'Yes, but remember that picture. Do we,' I asked earnestly, 'know what David is *really* like?'

'Oh, don't,' Rosemary protested. 'It's bad enough having been wrong about Sidney – don't tell me we've been wrong about David too.' She put the hyacinths in a planter and stood it on the window sill. 'Thank you so much, Sheila, I adore hyacinths but they never seem to grow for me. The bulb either goes all soggy or shrivels up and withers away. I'm hopeless with indoor plants. That cyclamen Delia and Alex bought me for my birthday – I only had it about a week and the leaves went yellow and it pined away and died. I *was* upset.'

'I expect you over watered it,' I said. 'Let the hyacinths dry right out before you give them any water and they should be fine.'

I spent Christmas day with the children, which was lovely, though Alice, overwhelmed by a multitude of presents, was a little grizzly towards the end of the day. It's a commonplace to say that children have too much of everything nowadays, but I'm sure they don't have the real and exquisite pleasure that we used to have as children when we finally achieved the one thing, toy, book or whatever, we'd been longing for all year. When Thea had put her to bed we sat around, stupefied by too much food, as one always is, until I finally roused myself and went back home to attend to my resentful animals, trying to make up for my absence by extra food. This satisfied Tris, who is a simple soul, but Foss blackmailed me into playing endless games with string, scrunched up tissue paper and bits of tinsel before he finally allowed me to make my weary way to bed.

Every Boxing Day Peter and I used to go to lunch with Jack and Rosemary and since his death I've kept up the comfortable tradition.

'Oh well,' Jack said as he filled my wine glass, 'Christmas is as far away now as ever it was.'

This was a remark he made every Boxing Day and Rosemary and I exchanged smiles. 'Now then,' he went on with his carving knife and fork poised over the splendid rib of beef. 'Well done for you Sheila, isn't it?'

As we ate our beef and Rosemary's exquisite Yorkshire pudding, talk turned, not surprisingly, to Sidney Middleton and his sudden death.

'Extraordinary way to do a person in,' Jack said. 'Must have been a really clever chap to have thought of that.'

'Marvellously simple, though,' I said. 'Didn't need any sort of force or special implement like a gun or a knife, or poison, even.'

'You'd have to know about flues and things,' Rosemary said. 'Not everyone would know about that.'

'So you think we're looking for someone who's got a stove like Sidney's?' I asked. 'That should narrow the field a bit.'

'No, no,' Jack said impatiently. 'It doesn't necessarily have to be the same *sort*. The general principle would be the same for any chimney. Once you stop the fumes escaping they're bound to be forced back, into the room. It could just as easily have been an ordinary fire, or a gas fire for that matter – it sometimes happens when those blasted starlings build their nests in the chimney.'

'Good heavens,' Rosemary said, 'is ours all right?'

'Yes, of course it is,' Jack said, 'we have the thing serviced every year and they check it then.'

'I'm going to get one of those carbon monoxide alarms, though,' I said, 'just to be on the safe side.'

'Good idea,' Rosemary said. 'Do have some more roast potatoes.'

'And all this stuff about the way he went on in Belgium in the war,' Jack went on. 'Dreadful way to behave, the man must have been a thoroughly bad sort to do something like that. After all, he was an officer, responsible for his men.'

'It's like an awful thing you read about in a book,' Rosemary said, 'not something that happens in real life.'

'Poor Bill Goddard was dreadfully upset,' I said, 'opening that letter after all these years. You can imagine the shock. And someone he'd always looked up to. Everyone did. There's never been the least breath of scandal about Sidney before all this came out.'

'I'm not so sure about that,' Jack said, reaching for the horseradish sauce. 'I've occasionally heard the odd whisper from a bloke I know in the City. Sailing a bit close to the wind sometimes.'

'Really? I've never heard that,' I said.

'I always dismissed it as gossip,' Jack said. 'A lot of old women as far as gossip's concerned, those City types. Mind you there was that business in his firm about insider trading. Not that Sidney had anything to do with that. Some young chap it was, got too clever, but they nabbed him in the end. Still, it leaves a nasty taste, that sort of thing.'

'Anyway,' Rosemary broke in, 'I wouldn't think Sidney would need to do anything crooked. He's always had pots of money.'

'Thanks to Joan,' I said. 'We always thought they were childhood sweethearts, all that sort of thing, but not according to your mother. She said he only married her for her money.'

'If Mother says so then it's probably true.' Rosemary laughed.

'Old Clive Wishart must have made a fortune from that agricultural machinery business,' Jack said, 'and Joan was his only child. There was a lot of money there.'

'She always seemed to worship him,' I said. 'Perhaps she did.'

'People are peculiar,' Rosemary said. 'Now then, how about pudding? I made a sherry trifle, lots of sherry because I thought we all needed bracing after the exhaustion of Christmas.'

That terrible dead week between Christmas and the New Year seemed to pass even more slowly than usual, but it was over at last and I was able to take down the cards and decorations that always seem to have outstayed their welcome by then. I spent New Year's Eve as I always do, quietly at home with the animals, occasionally switching on for a moment to watch the mechanical revels on television. People did very kindly ask me to their New Year celebrations but, as Rosemary once said, 'Think of the horror of a party you know you can't possibly leave until *after* midnight!'

I was in bed at midnight, reading, when Michael rang, as he always does, just to say Happy New Year.

'Oh, and by the way,' he added, 'I thought you'd like to know that we've got probate on Sidney Middleton's will, so Brian Thorpe and his mother now own the cottage at Withycombe so they'll be financially secure now.'

'I'm glad about that,' I said, 'but it doesn't really solve poor Brian's problem, does it?'

I ran into Roger at the weekend. He was loading shopping into the boot of his car.

'Hello,' I said, 'have they got you doing the supermarket run now?'

'Delia has a rotten cold and Alex has an ear infection, so Jilly's more or less housebound.'

'Oh poor little Alex, that's so painful, he must be feeling really miserable.'

'I've just been to collect his antibiotics so I hope it'll clear up soon.' He slammed the boot shut and went on, 'Sheila, if you have a few minutes to spare I'd like a word.'

'Yes, of course.'

'Let's sit in the car, shall we, it's bitterly cold.'

'I know,' I said as I got into the passenger seat, 'the wind blows into this car park straight off the sea!'

'It's about Sidney Middleton,' Roger said. 'I've been hearing rumours.'

'About that thing in the war?'

'That's right. My Sergeant Lister is the nephew of Ernie Shepherd, who's a friend of this Bill Goddard...'

'"And that's how tales do get about",' I quoted. 'I see.'

'So, after what you said about Sidney Middleton not being as universally popular as you thought he was, I wondered if you'd tell me now about this other person you mentioned and what sort of grudge *he* might have.'

'Oh dear. It *was* told to me in confidence.'

'And it will stay that way with me, you know that, just as long as it doesn't have any bearing on the case. It *is* a murder, after all.'

I sighed. 'I know. Oh, all right.'

I told Roger Brian's story and he looked thoughtful.

'And Middleton left them the cottage?'

'I think he more or less had to,' I said, 'he'd signed some sort of document years ago.'

'Mm, that gives this man Thorpe even

more of a motive, if there's property involved.'

'I don't think Brian's the sort of person – I mean, he wouldn't kill someone for property.'

'But he might do it as revenge for what happened in the past and what happened to his mother?'

'I suppose. But Roger,' I asked as a thought struck me, 'why do it *now*, after all these years? Why wait all this time?'

'Well, if, as you told me, he knew the cottage would come to him when Middleton died, and if the only way he can marry this woman is to put his mother in a home, then – well, you see...'

'Possibly. But – oh, I don't know – he's such a *nice* man!'

'But under an enormous amount of stress, and that makes people do uncharacteristic things.'

I thought of Brian's outburst at the funeral and how shocked I'd been. 'You're right, of course. Who knows what any of us would be capable of if we were really pushed?'

'And then there's this Bill Goddard. From what Sergeant Lister said he's been in a very agitated state.'

I told Roger about the letter and how moved I had been by it. 'He was dreadfully upset. I know Betty, that's his wife, was afraid he was going to have a breakdown...' I broke off.

'But Roger,' I went on, 'Bill is an old man. There's no way he could have done such a thing, however strongly he felt about it.'

'It doesn't take much strength to undo an inspection plate,' Roger said. 'Or to put it back again.'

I thought about Bill's solitary walks, but I couldn't bring myself to mention them to Roger.

I shook my head. 'I still can't believe it,' I said.

'Because you don't think it's possible?' Roger asked. 'Or because he's a friend and you're fond of him?'

'Both, I suppose. Are they – Brian and Bill – going to have to be interviewed?'

'I'd like to know where they were at the relevant time.'

'Well, look, it doesn't matter so much about Bill. He's been telling everyone about Sidney and the letter, but if you *could* manage not to let Brian know that you got his story from me...'

'I'd have been interviewing him anyway as a beneficiary under Middleton's will. And I'd have to ask him why he and his mother should have been left the cottage. I daresay the rest will come out if I approach it that way.'

'Oh, thank you, Roger.'

He smiled. 'We do try to protect our sources, you know, especially such valuable ones.'

'Will you let me know what you find out?'

'I daresay it may emerge. Oh, by the way, Sheila, I've been meaning to tell you. I've finally found a copy of *Three Brides*.'

Roger, like me is a Charlotte M. Yonge enthusiast.

'Oh, that's marvellous,' I said. 'That one is quite rare now. How did you find it? On the internet?'

'That's right – so lucky.'

'What do you think of it?'

'Mm. It will never be my favourite but it's got some splendid stuff in it. All that business with the drains and the casual way she killed off one of her main characters, poor Raymond, in the typhoid epidemic!'

'I know. Her females weren't supposed to have any interest in drains, it was thought unwomanly. But they pop up in most of the books, and not just hers. I've always wanted to write a paper on The Importance of Sanitation in the Victorian Novel, but I've never had the time.'

'Oh, I think you must. Well, I'd better be getting this antibiotic back to Alex. Thanks for the chat, Sheila.'

I got out of the car and went into the supermarket. By a strange coincidence I ran into Betty Goddard again.

'Hello, Betty, how's Bill? Is his bronchitis better?'

She looked up from examining a Buy One Get One Free display of tinned soup.

'Oh, hello, Sheila. Yes, Bill's much better – well, the bronchitis is, but he's not himself, not by a long chalk.'

'No,' I said, 'I suppose it's all been a dreadful strain.'

'He's been going down to the Legion practically every day and he comes back in quite a state. Telling everyone there about Sidney Middleton and then they all go on about it, over and over. Honestly, Sheila, when he first told you and then Fred I thought it would do him good to get it off his chest, but now the whole thing's getting right out of hand.'

'Oh dear.'

'He can't seem to talk about anything else – it's really shocking.'

'It must be very worrying for you.'

'Some days I'm at my wit's end. It can't be good for him.'

'What does Susan think?'

Susan is their grown up daughter. She and her husband and two children live in Bournemouth.

'They've been away. They went to Trevor's people for Christmas and stayed on a bit, so I couldn't have a talk with her straight away. But, of course, they've had to come back for the children's school now. I rang her yesterday and she said to bring Bill down and stay with them for a bit.'

'That sounds like a very good idea,' I said. 'A change of scene might be just what he needs.'

'He likes to see the children,' Betty said, 'well, we both do, and I like the shops. Trevor said he'd come and fetch us at the weekend, and I'm sure the Nortons would look after the house for us while we're away.'

'I think you should go. It'll do you good as well.'

When I got outside the sky was iron grey and it was very cold.

'Looks like snow,' the man collecting up the trolleys said cheerfully.

'Oh, I do hope not,' I said, thinking of all the inconveniences snow always brings. But

184

as I drove away the first flakes began to fall and by the time I got home a white, whirling mass was blown into my face by the wind as I got out of the car.

13

The snow was quite deep by the next morning. It looked absolutely beautiful, of course, the trees and hills brilliant white against the iron grey sky that promised more to come, but I am too old now to take delight in the aesthetic qualities of snow. My thoughts were more prosaic: would the electricity go off, and would it be possible to drive my car up the lane? I spent a considerable amount of the day staring morosely out of the window, hoping for some gleam of sun that would melt the wretched stuff. Tris, however, loves the snow and made little forays outside, scratching away on the lawn and inspecting with interest the tracks made by other, wilder creatures in the night. Foss would have nothing to do with it. Having satisfied himself that there was snow outside *every* door, he gave me a glance of deep disappointment and took himself up to my bed where he spent the day curled up in a disapproving ball.

The snow melted a little the next day and

then it froze, bringing new hazards. The following day more snow fell and I thought I really must try to clear a path for the postman and the milkman who had been nobly making deliveries. I'm not very good with a shovel – and this was a heavy, spear-shaped implement that had belonged to my father and was always used by him for such tasks – and I was just pausing for breath when a van churned its way slowly up the lane, stopped outside the gate and Brian got out.

'Here,' he called out as he approached, 'let me do that.'

'Are you sure?' I said, relinquishing the shovel gratefully. 'Can I make you a cup of something?'

'Tea would be nice.'

I went back into the kitchen, put the kettle on and got out the cake tin. After a while there was a knock at the back door.

'I'll leave my boots outside, shall I?' Brian asked, shaking the powdered snow off his jacket.

'Come on in,' I said. 'Tea's ready.'

'I came to see about those shelves,' he said. 'That's if you still want them.'

'I most certainly do. Even though I hardly ever buy new books these days I've still got piles of them sitting on the floor in the dining-room now! Do have a piece of fruit cake, or there's some sponge if you'd rather.'

'Right, then, I'll go and measure up in a moment. It's just that this is usually a quiet time for me. Most people don't think about having things done just after Christmas, they seem to wait for the Spring.'

We chatted for a while on general topics, quite easily, just as though Brian's outburst last time we had spoken had never happened. Then, out of the blue, he said, 'The police came to see me yesterday.'

'Really? What for?'

'About Middleton. This Inspector said he had to talk to everyone who benefited under his will.'

'Yes, of course.'

'Because it's a murder enquiry, you see. So I had to tell him why we got the cottage and some money.'

'I see.'

Brian crumbled the slice of fruit cake on his plate. 'I said, "I suppose that means I'm a suspect, then?"'

'Surely not!'

'Well, you can see how they'd think so. But he was very polite – didn't say yes or no.'

'I'm sure you're not the only person to

have a reason to kill him,' I said, 'especially now it's all coming out about what a horrible person he was. I expect the police are talking to lots of people.' I poured us both another cup of tea and went on, 'Anyway, I'm so glad you've got the cottage. It's some sort of security for you both.'

'I saw his son a while back,' Brian said. 'He came to see me.'

'He came to see you?' I echoed in surprise. 'David?'

'Yes.'

'Why? I mean, what for?'

'He knew about Mother and me.'

'Really?'

'He said he was glad we had the cottage and the money.'

'Good heavens.'

'Yes, I was really taken aback. Said he'd known for some time. He was going to tell me more, I think, when Mother came in. She'd been lying down, having a bit of a rest when he came. As you can imagine, I was worried how she'd take it, him being there. She's not good with strangers – well *you* know that.'

'So what happened?'

'I couldn't believe it. She really took to him, right from the start, she's never done that before to anyone.'

'How extraordinary.'

'He was wonderful with her, very gentle and unthreatening. He seemed to know, without being told, how she was. He just chatted to her. Not about anything special, the weather, the ornaments she had on the mantelpiece, things like that. And she loved it. I haven't seen her like that for years. She even offered to make him a cup of tea, but he said he couldn't stay. But he asked if he could come again. He said that we had a lot to talk about. I don't know what he meant by that. But Mother was really pleased. Said to let us know when he was coming and she'd make her special apple cake. I could not believe it.'

'It's quite extraordinary. I wonder what he wants to talk to you about?'

'Must be something about his father, I suppose, if he wouldn't say anything while Mother was there.'

'And he didn't seem upset or put out about it?' I asked.

'No, not at all. Quite the contrary in a way. I mean, from his tone and the way he went on.'

'I wonder if he *will* come and see you again?'

'Oh, I think he will. He seemed quite positive about that.' He got up. 'Well, I'd better get measured up for those shelves instead of rabbiting on here.' He stood there for a moment and then, with a sort of effort, he said, 'Mrs Malory, I do appreciate being able to talk to you about all this. I talk to Margaret, of course, but she's sort of involved and I try to be careful about what I say for fear of upsetting her.'

'I'm sure she understands,' I said.

'Oh yes, of course she does,' he agreed hastily, 'it's just that I really don't want her to feel hurt about things.'

'She's probably tougher than you think,' I said. 'But I'm always happy to listen whenever you want to talk.'

'I felt rather mean,' I said to Thea, 'when he thanked me for listening and I'd been pumping him like mad out of curiosity.'

'Still,' Thea said, 'whatever your motive, I'm sure you're helping him. But how extraordinary about David Middleton!'

'I know. I can't imagine what he's up to.'

'It sounds so unlike him.'

'Yes, and the bit about Brian's mother,' I said, 'now that really *is* weird! I mean, I told you what she was like with me and I reckon

I'm reasonably unthreatening.'

'Have you seen David recently?' she asked.

'No, not since the funeral. I told you I saw Bridget, didn't I, and how she avoided me. I believe they've got the boys back home so that should make her happy – though I still can't imagine what made David change his mind and yank them out of boarding school, after all he's said about the *advantages* they're getting there.'

'Perhaps he did it for Bridget's sake,' Thea said. 'You know, if she was upset about Sidney's death for some reason.'

'It doesn't sound like the David I know to consider Bridget's feelings, and anyway, why should *she* be so upset about Sidney?'

Thea shrugged. 'Who knows. The whole thing seems to me to be full of contradictions – people not being what they seem, or acting out of character.'

'True. Still, the one thing I can't see is David Middleton playing happy families!'

But that, in fact, is exactly what I did see the following Saturday. I'd gone with Rosemary to the big garden centre near Taunton – the one where we'd seen Brian and his Margaret.

'I know it's stupid to go to places like that at the weekend,' Rosemary said, 'it's bound to be crowded, but Mother wants a couple of new houseplants, and they do have the best selection, and being Mother she wants them *now*.'

'That's all right,' I said. 'If we go early we might just manage to get a table and have lunch there.'

We found the plants ('She wanted one of those striped African violets and a *yellow* begonia – Can you see one anywhere? These are all pink') and went over to the café which was already nearly full. Rosemary, loaded down with plants, found an empty table while I went to queue for the food. As I stood there I looked around and to my immense surprise saw, in a corner, David, Bridget and their two boys, all eating toasted sandwiches and drinking Coca Cola, just like any other, normal family having a day out. I was so absorbed in this amazing sight that the person behind me in the queue had to touch me on the shoulder when it was my turn to be served.

'Don't look now,' I said as I put the tray down on the table, 'but you'll never guess who's sitting over there in the far corner.'

Rosemary craned her neck discreetly. 'Good Heavens,' she said. 'I don't believe it, David Middleton being a good husband

and father!'

'I know, isn't it extraordinary? Acting out of character again. You know I told you about him turning up at Brian's.'

'Most peculiar.'

'And then there was that picture. Did Roger like it, by the way?'

'Yes, he loved it.' She wiped the icing from her Danish pastry off her fingers. 'Perhaps David has a split personality, sort of Jekyll and Hyde stuff.'

'Possibly,' I said thoughtfully, 'or else we've been wrong about him all the time, just as we were wrong about Sidney.'

The group in the corner got up to leave and I heard David say, 'Come on you lot, else we'll be late for the film and have to go to a *museum* or something!' in a voice I'd never heard him use before – cheerful, jokey and affectionate. Rosemary heard him too and looked at me with raised eyebrows.

'Well, wonders will never cease. And they all looked so happy!'

'I know. Wasn't that nice? Peculiar, but nice.'

There was one more surprise to come about David Middleton. I was sitting in the surgery waiting to see Dr Macdonald when

Myra Norton came in. I fervently hoped she hadn't seen me because I didn't feel up to coping with her tidal wave of talk, but she came over straight away and took the chair next to mine.

'Hello, fancy seeing you here. Nothing wrong, I hope? I've got to see Dr Hurst about my varicose veins, really shocking they are, and I don't fancy those elastic stockings. I tried them once but they felt really *funny*, if you know what I mean, so I didn't persevere. You'd think in this day and age – I mean, when they can put a man on the moon – they'd be able to do something, wouldn't you? I suppose it'll just be more pills. Honestly, I seem to take so many – and so does Jim, you should see us at breakfast time counting them out. I said if you turned us upside down we'd rattle!'

'I know, it is awful, isn't it.'

'So how about you?'

'Oh, nothing much, just routine checks, blood pressure and so on.'

'Jim's blood pressure goes up and down like a yo-yo. I said to him, "You ought to get one of those monitor things you can have strapped to your wrist", but he wouldn't. Well, you know what men are like, won't do anything to help themselves. Betty was saying just the same about Bill and his bronchitis.'

'Are they back from Bournemouth yet? I've been meaning to call.'

'No, they're still there. Well, they were coming back last week, but with all that snow it would have been a difficult journey. Betty said they could go back by train but Susan wouldn't hear of it and said they should wait until Trevor, that's their son-in-law, is free to drive them.'

'I'm sure the break will do them good.'

'Oh yes. Bournemouth's very nice, it used to be very select. We had some really nice holidays there. The sand's lovely for the kiddies and I always used to say that the shops are almost as good as London.'

'Well, I do hope that Bill will be quite recovered when they get back.'

'So do I. Between ourselves I was quite worried about him, not his usual self at all, and I could tell Betty was really upset about how he was.'

'I'm sure she was.'

'Out walking at all hours, no wonder he got that bronchitis. I said to Jim, "He shouldn't be out in all winds and weathers like that" and Jim agreed. But you could tell he wasn't right, very uptight, if you know what I mean. Such a dreadful thing to have happened, and right out of the blue like that!'

'I know it was a terrible shock to him.'

'Well, it would be, wouldn't it. Terrible!'

'We must hope that the little break will have helped him get over it.'

'Actually, Betty told me he was much better after that man's son came to see him.'

'David Middleton? Really? Are you sure?'

'Oh yes, Betty said she was as surprised as anything when he turned up and asked to see Bill.'

'I can see that she might be.'

'Just stood on the doorstep, Betty told me, and said, "Do you think Bill would see me?" Well, she asked him in of course and I don't know what happened because she left them to it, but she said that when he left – and she said he was really nice to her and thanked her ever so much for letting him see Bill – Bill was much more his old self.'

'Really?'

'I think she was surprised because from what she told me he wasn't usually like that.'

'No.'

'Very stand-offish, she said, kept himself to himself. So when he was so friendly, well, she couldn't believe it was the same person.

Mind you,' she leaned towards me and spoke confidentially, 'after what happened it was the least he could do, going to see Bill, I mean. Not that that would make it all right, of course, but I suppose he felt he had to do something in the circumstances.'

'Yes. I'm glad that Bill felt better after seeing him.'

'Oh yes. Betty said he quite perked up – ate all his lunch and had the best night's sleep he'd had for a long time.'

'That was splendid.'

'I think we all feel better for a good night's sleep. Jim sleeps like a log no matter what, but if I'm the least bit upset I'll toss and turn all night and then the next day I'm fit for nothing.'

'I know, it is awful, isn't it.'

'What I always say is...'

But I never knew what pearl of wisdom she was going to produce because Dr Hurst appeared just then and called her in.

I sat in a sort of daze, turning over in my mind all the newly revealed facets of David Middleton's personality, unable to reconcile this amiable figure with the taciturn, disagreeable man I thought I knew. I was so lost in thought that Dr Macdonald had to repeat my name several times before I heard him and meekly followed him into his consulting room, where, not surprisingly, my blood pressure was slightly up.

14

'Are you going to Christine's dinner party?' Rosemary asked.

I groaned. 'I suppose I'll have to. I made an excuse last time, said I had a cold, and I *know* she didn't believe me and was quite offended.'

I must say, dinner parties aren't really my scene. When Peter was alive I dutifully gave them, as one does, for business contacts, but, left to ourselves, we both preferred to see our friends casually in ones and twos. As a widow and a 'spare woman' things were more complicated, since, then, a suitable 'spare man' had to be found. However in recent years, in such a geriatric society as ours in Taviscombe the number of widows has made such situations largely irrelevant and there is no longer the obligation to match up dinner guests like animals in the Ark.

Christine, though, was the exception. Her dinner parties were resolutely formal so that I was only invited when her brother

Desmond, whose wife had died some years ago ('And glad to,' said Rosemary) came to visit and I was deemed a suitable and safe (she was under the misapprehension that Desmond was something of a 'catch') dinner companion for him. Actually another reason I dreaded Christine's parties was that Desmond was one of the most mind-numbingly boring people I have ever met, the sort of man whose conversation induces a sort of cataleptic trance in his listener.

Because Francis was an accountant too, Jack and Rosemary were usually invited to these dinner parties – one of the few things that made the occasions more bearable for me, though I did have to make an effort to avoid Rosemary's eye when Christine did or said something particularly awful.

'Presumably Desmond is staying with them again,' Rosemary said.

'Don't, it doesn't bear thinking of. Oh how I wish I were brave enough to *really* offend her, so that I'd never have to go there again! I mean, it wouldn't break my heart if I never saw her or Francis *or* Desmond ever again. It's just a sort of social convention that's stopping me.'

'That and the fact that it would be almost impossible actually to set out to offend someone, don't you think?' Rosemary said thoughtfully. 'It's something that must happen by accident or not at all.'

Another reason for hating Christine's parties that one is also expected to dress formally, and with the sort of life I lead my wardrobe is full of tops and skirts with only one or two proper frocks. I took them both out and looked at them. The regulation little black dress had definitely seen better days and did (I had to admit) strain a bit over the hips. The other, an olive green silk shirt-waister, when held up against me, made me, with my winter pallor, look like some creature that had been shut away from the light for several months. Even if it was only for dreary Desmond my pride wouldn't allow me to appear in public in either of those.

'Well,' I said to Foss who, as usual had followed me upstairs in case I was going to be engaged in something interesting, 'I'm jolly well not going to *buy* anything new, just for Christine's horrible party.'

I delved into the wardrobe in the forlorn hope of finding something that would 'do' and came up with a black velvet skirt, relic of what now seemed like a bygone age when such garments were fashionable, and an equally old 'dressy' white blouse. I decided that with a wide belt to hide the safety pin that was needed to accommodate my expanded waistline I could just about get away with it. The blouse was all right as long as I didn't do anything strenuous, which seemed unlikely in the circumstances.

'Retro,' I said to Foss. 'It's all the rage now.'

He gave me a look of contempt and began to sharpen his claws on the carpet while I bore the clothes away to see what dry cleaning could do for them.

I tried not to arrive at Christine's too early, but the taxi turned up exactly on time (I didn't drive myself because I thought that I might need a reasonable amount of alcohol to see me through the evening), so I was the first one there. Except for Desmond, of course. Francis gave me a glass of sherry and, fortified by this, I plunged in.

'Did you have a good trip down from London?' I asked Desmond, giving him the opening I knew he wanted. His eyes lit up and he began his usual mile by mile description of the journey, which enabled me to switch off, only odd phrases coming through ('Absolute chaos at the Reading turn-off … road-works at Leigh Delamere

... three mile tail-back at the Almondsbury interchange...') so that, familiar as I was with the narrative, I only had to fix an expression of interest on my face and make soothing comments ('How ghastly ... dreadful!... The M5 is getting worse by the day!...') in the rare moments when he paused for breath.

Fortunately Rosemary and Jack arrived fairly soon and the conversation became more general. Knowing Christine's usual obsession with numbers, I was interested to see who her other two guests would be. They were David and Bridget Middleton. I suppose I really shouldn't have been surprised, since David was yet another accountant, but I hadn't realised that they were part of Christine's 'circle'.

They both looked terrific. Bridget was totally unlike her usual mousey self. She was wearing an elegant frock in soft raspberry red (a colour I had never seen her in before) which accentuated the darkness of her hair (could she have had a rinse?) And she positively shone with happiness. She greeted me with what appeared to be great pleasure – it was as if her previous avoidance of me had never been. David, too, looked a different person. I'd noticed in the garden centre how relaxed and easy he was, so different from the slightly surly difficult person I thought I knew and now he was – well, no other word for it – charming.

At the dinner table I was pleased to find that I was seated next to David. True I had Desmond on my other side but years of experience had taught me how to cope with that. While Christine, like a good hostess, devoted herself first to David on her left, I concentrated on the food, while blocking out Desmond's account of some new export regulation. He was somewhere in the middle order at the Board of Trade, or whatever it's called now, and his frequent trips to Brussels gave him lots of lovely new material for his endless monologues.

The first course was a game terrine, which was all right since Christine had obviously bought it in from our splendid deli. The main course was my real source of worry since Christine liked to think of herself as an innovative cook. I'm sure that in the hands of an expert chef squid cooked in its own ink is a rare delicacy. Christine's version gave me nightmares for days after. This time I was relieved to see that although the rack of lamb was fashionably pink (not to my taste) and the broccoli and fennel were, as usual, underdone, they were at least edible.

'I'm sure you agree?' Desmond was saying.

'Oh yes, absolutely,' I replied vigorously.

'So of course,' Desmond said triumphantly, 'I referred them to the EC 1999 order, sub-section 23 and that settled the matter.'

'How splendid.'

Finally, after what seemed like an age, Christine turned to Jack on her other side, poor Rosemary was lumbered with Desmond, and I finally got to talk to David.

After a few commonplaces about the weather and so on, I said, 'I did so love that painting of yours of the moor in winter. I don't think I've seen anything that sums up the place and the season so perfectly.'

He gave me a shy (*shy*, David Middleton!) smile and said, 'That's really kind of you – it's the time I love the best and I did so want to try and capture it.'

'You certainly did that,' I said warmly. 'As you may know Rosemary bought it and she felt the same way as I did. I had no idea that you were an artist.'

'Oh I wouldn't say that,' he said modestly (David Middleton, *modest!*). 'I just enjoy messing about with paints – only water-colours, I've never attempted oils! I'm very much an amateur. Audrey Fisher persuaded me to put it in the exhibition, so I did, just to make up the numbers really.'

'I was wondering,' I said, 'if by any chance you have any other painting you might be willing to sell? Only my cousin Hilda, who loves Exmoor, has a birthday coming up soon – it's her eightieth so I wanted something really special for her and one of your paintings would be absolutely perfect!'

'Well, I don't know...' He spoke hesitantly. 'I'm not sure if there's anything good enough.'

'I'm sure there must be.'

'If you'd like to come and have a look?'

'That would be wonderful.'

We arranged a day and a time and I began to feel that the evening was not being such a dead loss after all.

'Did you talk to the new David?' I asked Rosemary when she came round the next morning to compare notes.

'I know – a completely different person! Isn't it extraordinary? And Bridget too, she looked positively glamorous. It's almost as if Sidney dying released them from some sort of spell, like in a fairy tale. I long to know what's *happened*.'

'It really is very odd,' I said. 'I wasn't able to do more than exchange a few pleasantries yesterday, but on Saturday I'm going over there to choose a picture to give to Hilda for her birthday.'

'Oh good. If anyone can find out what's been going on you can!'

The house, about ten miles out on the Taunton side of Taviscombe, was handsome and substantial, built in the 1930s. What estate agents call 'a family home', though they do not specify what sort of family. There was a large garden, leading to a paddock with stabling for the statutory children's pony. The whole thing looked like an illustration for a book by Enid Blyton.

David answered the door. 'Hello, Sheila, do come in. I'm afraid Bridget and the boys aren't here,' he said, leading me through into the drawing-room. 'James has a music lesson and Tony's got a rugby practice.'

'Oh I know, parents are simply chauffeurs nowadays, ferrying the children from A to B.'

He laughed. 'Do let me get you a coffee, anyway.'

'That would be lovely.'

The drawing room was handsomely if conventionally furnished. There was a piano in one corner (for James's music presumably) and large-screen television (for Tony to watch the rugby?) in another. There were several photographs of the boys and one of Bridget, though none of David – or, indeed, of his father. There were a few watercolours and mezzotints on the walls, though none of David's. I was just studying a particularly fine Birkett Foster rural scene when David came back into the room with a tray.

'This is beautiful,' I said. 'How lovely to have a Birkett Foster of your very own.'

He smiled. 'A wicked indulgence,' he said. 'As was the David Cox.' He indicated a small picture beside the fireplace, a river scene, with a wonderfully dramatic stormy sky.

'Goodness! That *is* a treasure,' I exclaimed as I went over to look at it more closely.

'I pretended to myself that they were investments,' David said laughing. 'But I knew that I'd never bring myself to sell them!'

'They're wonderful,' I said. 'Does Bridget share your enthusiasm?'

'No, music's her line, that's where James gets it from. But she's very understanding.'

The coffee was in a cafetiere and the cups were elegant bone china. I was impressed.

'None of your pictures here,' I said.

'Good heavens no – not in the same room as those two masters! No, I have a sort of studio upstairs. I keep them there.'

While we drank our coffee we talked for a while about the English school of water-colour painting, about which David was very knowledgeable. Fortunately my father had also been a keen amateur collector so I was able to keep my end up, more or less. After a while David stood up and said, 'Well, if you'd really like to see my stuff we'll go up then.'

The studio was right at the top of the house and I was a little out of breath by the time we got there. It was a large room, the attic really, running the full length of the house. There were two skylights in the roof that gave excellent light, an easel, a large trestle table and a cabinet containing a variety of paints, papers and other artistic impedimenta. A very professional room, but neat and well-ordered with the scrupulous tidiness of an amateur artist. There were a few pictures on the walls but mostly they were propped up on the floor with their faces turned to the wall.

'What a marvellous room,' I said.

'Another indulgence,' he said. 'I'm very lucky to be able to pursue my hobby like this.'

'How do you work? Do you make rough sketches out on the moor and then work them up when you get home?'

'Sometimes. But sometimes, when the weather's right, I like to do the whole thing out there. I love the moor.'

'Yes,' I said, looking at some of the paintings hanging on the wall, 'I can see that.'

We stood in silence for a moment, and I think we were both startled by the ringing of a mobile phone. He muttered an apology and held it to his ear.

'I'm so sorry,' he said. 'I'll take it downstairs. Make yourself at home – have a look round.'

The pictures on the walls were all of the moor in Winter, all as fine and evocative as the first one we had seen at the exhibition. There was a spareness and simplicity about them all, and he had captured the feeling of the place, the bare bones of the landscape, and the season. I turned my attention to the ones on the floor. Some of these showed the moor in Spring, the delicate, pale green tips of the whortleberries, the first hint of growth on the ling, the slow unfurling of the bracken, all done with great sensitivity of observation. One picture showed the spot I always think of as 'my' bit of the moor – down in the combe of Weirwater where the stream runs clear and fast, overhung with small rowan trees, where the stone-chat's call is the only sound. It would have been fatally easy to have made it a conventionally 'pretty' scene, but David had reduced it to a minimum in such a way that he had captured the very essence of the place without a hint of sentimentality. It was a really impressive piece of work and the picture I knew I must have to keep for myself.

Almost any of the others would have delighted Hilda, it was hard to choose. But as I continued to turn over the pictures I came upon one that was not a landscape. It was the portrait of an elderly woman. David wasn't as good at catching a likeness and the general style was more stiff, less fluid, than his landscapes. Nevertheless I still recognised the sitter. It was his mother, Joan Middleton.

It was a picture that was painful to look at. Not because of the quality of the work, but because of the emotion on the subject's face and, by association, the emotion of the person who painted it. There was pain there, and fear, and a sort of hopelessness that almost made me turn away, since I felt I was looking at something I should not have seen. But I couldn't help looking, trying to relate this portrait to the Joan I had known – quiet, unobtrusive, placid, even. But apparently, like everything else I had thought I knew about the Middletons, totally wrong.

'I'm sorry, I thought I'd put that away.' David was standing in the doorway.

I turned quickly, flustered. 'I'm so sorry – it was with the others...'

His face closed down and for a moment he was the David I used to know, then he recovered himself and said lightly, 'It was just an experiment. I'm not any good at portraits.'

'On the contrary,' I said. 'It seems to me that you've caught your subject very well.' I moved towards him. 'David, I'm so sorry, I'd no idea...'

He shook his head, without saying anything, but I went on, 'Since Sidney died, it's become perfectly obvious that we never really knew him – or you, or (now I've seen this) poor Joan. How can we have been so blind?'

He gave a short laugh. 'He was clever,

devious and – well, people see what they expect to see. Sidney Middleton was a good man, generous, he gave to charity, he supported good causes. He was friendly and easy with people. People liked him, of course they did when he put himself out to charm them. All the time. But not at home. Not to us. He was selfish, arrogant, domineering, ruled our lives, so that we were too frightened to rebel. My mother gave up almost immediately. He married her for her money and treated her like dirt. Bullied her, struck her sometimes. I tried to stand up for her, I tried to speak out, but who would believe me when all the world knew what a wonderful person he was? And, as I got older, he'd built up this persona for me – the bossy son, who tried to bully a poor old man – and everyone believed that. I got a job down here, while he was still in London, and I thought I was free. But he retired here, back to his roots, he said and everyone said how nice. But it was so that he could go on controlling me and my family.'

He closed his eyes as if to shut out a painful memory. 'When he died, it was wonderful, though even now sometimes I can't be sure the old devil is really dead.'

15

'That's more or less what Brian said at the funeral,' I said.

He looked startled. 'Brian? You know about Brian?'

'It's a long story, but yes, I know about Brian.'

'It was just about the last straw,' he said. 'Finding out about that after *he* died. It more or less destroyed me. To think that he'd ruined other people's lives like he'd ruined ours. Thank God he'd had to make provision for them – at least they've got the cottage and some money, but nothing can ever make up for what he did to them. That's why I had to go and see him. That poor woman!'

'Brian told me how wonderful you were with her.'

'All those years,' he said, 'trying to support my own mother. I knew how fragile she must be. I need to go back and have a proper talk with him – try and make him understand that I had no idea – try to make some sort of amends.'

'Is that why you went to see Bill Goddard?' I asked.

'Yes. I heard what had happened there and I was horrified! The way that man's evil spread, like throwing a stone into a pond – so many terrible effects.'

'How awful.'

He was silent for a moment, then he said, 'One thing that was really frightening. I told you how he created this persona for me – the bossy, domineering son – he built it up so cleverly that I almost found myself becoming that person. Can you imagine that! My poor Bridget, in the end she never knew where she stood with me. I had these mood swings; it must have been dreadful for her. And having the boys sent away to school, it upset her so much. But I had to, you see.'

'Had to?'

'I had to get them away. They were just at the age when they were beginning to be influenced by him. He gave them things, expensive presents, money. He was trying to turn them against me. I couldn't have that. I sent them away to school and I made sure that he never saw them in the holidays, just as I tried to keep Bridget away as well.'

'Didn't she know how things were?' I asked.

He shook his head. 'In the beginning I just couldn't. It seemed a shameful thing – and there was my mother, too. Somehow I didn't want her to know about that, it was too painful. And, as time went on it became more and more difficult to say anything.'

'But she knows now?'

'Oh yes. When he died I told her everything. She was very upset, we both were, it was a really traumatic time for both of us.'

I remembered how they were at the funeral. 'Yes,' I said. 'I can imagine.'

'My poor girl. I don't know if I can ever make it up to her.'

'She loves you,' I said. 'She's so happy now, you can see that just by looking at her. Not just because you're back to your real self, but because you've *told* her – you've shared it with her.'

'I wanted to keep it all from her,' he said, 'to spare her the knowledge...'

I smiled. 'Women would rather know,' I said, 'believe me. They don't want to be spared, they're hurt when you shut them out.'

'You're probably right. As I said, she was very upset at first, especially about Brian and Bill Goddard. She felt people were talking about us and she couldn't face them, but gradually she's realised that it's OK. And now, she's a different person. We both are. It's as if some terrible *thing* has been lifted from our lives and we can be ourselves again.'

He looked round the studio. 'This was the only escape I had, the only place where I could be myself. That's the great thing about painting, you can lose yourself completely in what you're doing.'

'You have a remarkable gift,' I said.

He shook his head. 'No, I'm just an average amateur, but it's been my lifeline.'

'It's not just the technical ability you have,' I said, 'it's the observation behind the pictures that make them special. You really seem to be in tune with nature, if that doesn't sound too banal.'

'The moor is a wonderful place. That feeling of space, being able to step outside the world, the way it cleanses you – that was so important to me. I suppose that's why I like it best in Winter, when it's stripped down to bare essentials and the wind scours away all the bad things and you're left with what is *real*.' He stopped abruptly and gave a self-conscious laugh. 'I'm sorry, I didn't mean to go on like that. But I think you understand.'

'Yes,' I said, ' I've drawn comfort from it in my time.'

'I want to try and do *something* to put right some of the things he did. I know I can never undo those things, but I feel I've got to do what I can for Brian and his mother and for Bill Goddard and God knows how many other people he's injured in ways I may never know about.'

'But none of it is your fault,' I said. 'You mustn't think that. You are even more of a victim than any of them.'

'But that's why I must try to make some sort of amends, because *I* understand how hurt they've been and how their lives have been affected.'

'What can you do?'

'The very least I can do is talk to them, tell them how it was for me and how I know what they must have gone through and how *sorry* I am.' He looked at me earnestly. 'I can, I suppose, simply apologise. Do you think that's silly?'

I shook my head. 'No. An apology, given as you would give it, would mean a lot.'

I turned back to the picture of his mother. 'I think she would be proud of you,' I said, 'and so happy that you're free at last.'

He smiled sadly. 'Too late for her.'

'But all those years, you must have been her lifeline, remember that.'

I chose my picture of Weirwater and a lovely painting of Molland Common in Winter for Hilda.

'It's very like the one Rosemary bought,' I said, holding it up to admire it. 'It was a Christmas present for her son-in-law, Roger Eliot, you know, the...' I broke off, embarrassed.

'The policeman who's investigating my father's death,' David said. 'Yes, he mentioned it when he came to see me. Apparently he liked it very much.'

'Roger is very civilised,' I said, flustered by the turn the conversation had taken. 'He reads the Victorian novelists.'

David smiled. 'Really,' he said. 'A man of many parts.'

'Did he,' I enquired tentatively, 'give you any idea how the investigation was going?'

'No. I didn't ask. He just asked me the sort of questions you'd expect – where was I on the night in question, that sort of thing. Not that I was any help. I was here, at home all evening with Bridget, but I don't expect that would count as an alibi.'

'Oh well,' I said hastily, 'I don't imagine he thought you needed one.'

'Oh, I'm sure I'm a suspect,' David said, 'and why not? I hated my father and I'm delighted he's dead. My only regret is that it didn't happen years ago.'

When I got home, after I'd let the animals out, I spent a long time deciding where to hang my picture. Eventually I hung it above my desk so that I could see it when I looked up, seeking inspiration. Only then did I allow myself to think about my extraordinary conversation with David. It was very disconcerting. Just when I thought I'd finally reached the truth about the real Sidney Middleton some new strata of horribleness was revealed. I had no doubt that what David had told me was the truth, but the enormity of what he'd suggested was difficult to grasp. I could just about accept that Sidney had been a monstrous hypocrite who'd deceived us all these years – the revelations after his death made that only too obvious – but what David had suggested about his father's dealings with him were almost beyond my comprehension. But his whole manner and the obvious pain it had cost him to tell me his story made it impossible for me not to believe him.

I thought of Joan and of how (now I came to think of it) I'd hardly ever seen her alone, hardly ever had a conversation with her except in Sidney's company. She'd seemed simply shy and not very bright, a mousy little woman with a clever, devoted husband. Had she known about Brian and his mother, was that an extra pain she'd had to bear? How had she kept up appearances for so long? Can fear become a habit? Perhaps one can become accustomed to anything, and, of course, she had had David to protect. And all the time Sidney had basked in his popularity, been accepted as a charming, generous man, a pillar, as they say, of the community.

Suddenly I remembered an incident. It was the day of their Ruby wedding. I had called in at the hotel near Taunton early to drop off a present before the party itself. As I approached the Oak Room where the party was to be held I heard Sidney talking to one of the hotel staff. I couldn't hear the words, but I gathered that he was complaining about something, complaining very forcefully. I remember being surprised because I'd never heard him use that tone of voice before, but I assumed that the error had been of major proportions and that he had wanted everything to be perfect on this particular day. But now, in my mind's eye, I saw Joan, sitting by the window of the room. She was crouched forward, her arms clasped about her shoulders, rocking back and forth. I suppose I'd been so surprised at Sidney's outburst that I'd forgotten that picture of Joan. I backed away and left the hotel and when I arrived at the party I found Sidney in great form, welcoming the guests, making the occasion a great success. Everyone said how marvellous it had been and what a pity it was that Joan was so shy and didn't exert herself more.

I got up from my chair, wanting to shake off my thoughts, to wipe out the memory. I went out into the kitchen and, as I mechanically started to cut up some food for the animals, it was suddenly borne in upon me that Sidney Middleton had been murdered and that David had had an overwhelming motive for killing him. Not just David, though. Brian, too, had suffered intolerable misery and so, to a lesser degree, had Bill Goddard. I put down the scissors and thought about it. David said that he had no alibi. I wondered about the other two. Somehow I didn't want to know. Like David and Brian I was glad that the man was dead and I didn't want Roger to catch whoever was responsible.

Actually I saw Roger the very next day. I'd had to go into the bank to sort out a query on my statement – it's impossible to deal with these things by phone now – and I was feeling confused, as I always do when I have to deal with figures, so I didn't see him at first.

'Hello, Sheila,' he said, 'you seem miles away!'

'It all comes from not being numerate,' I said, stuffing the statement into my handbag. 'Anything to do with figures and a shutter comes down in my mind. It's very depressing.'

He laughed. 'Come and have a coffee and cheer up I've got half an hour before I need to get back.'

In a way, feeling as I did about Sidney's death, I didn't really want to have a chat with Roger just then and for a while I kept the conversation strictly to family matters.

'How's Delia?' I asked. 'I feel I should be getting all the information I can for when Alice is that age. I'm quite sure it will be quite different from the way it was with Michael.'

'All I can say,' Roger said, wiping the icing sugar from his Belgian bun off his fingers, 'is make the most of *now*. The older they get the more difficult it is! We've just had to redecorate her room because it wasn't cool enough for her to invite her friends round. It's all mauve now, mauve and silver. Mauve, apparently is the new pink – no, don't ask! I'm just echoing my daughter.'

I laughed. 'I'll bear it in mind.'

'And as for this mobile phone business. I held out against it for ages, but we had to give in the end. The theory is that at least they can get in touch if they're in trouble, but, of course, what they really use them for is chatting to their friends. Can you explain it to me? Delia went to a sleep-over (dreadful phrase) with her friend Abbie. From what I can gather they chattered away all night instead of sleeping and then the moment she got home, she was onto the phone to her talking away as if she hadn't seen her for a month!'

'Oh dear. And what about Alex?'

'Football mad like the rest of them, but I can cope with that. It's poor Jilly who has to deal with the muddy shirts and boots...' He broke off and then he said, 'Sheila, about Sidney Middleton.'

'Yes?'

'I've been trying to check where people were, the night he died.'

'Oh,' I said, trying to sound casual, 'and what did you find out?'

'Neither Bill Goddard or Brian Thorpe had an alibi. They both said they were at home.'

'Well,' I said, 'Brian couldn't leave his mother and Bill Goddard is an old man with a bad chest infection. Where else would they be?'

He looked at me quizzically. 'Where indeed?'

I smiled but didn't say anything.

'I went to see David Middleton,' Roger said.

'Oh yes?'

'Since he has the strongest motive after all.'

'But he didn't inherit anything,' I said quickly. 'It's all in trust for the boys.'

'Might that not be a motive?'

'Well, yes, in a way,' I replied, 'but surely, by the time the boys were of age, Sidney might very well have died of natural causes.'

'True. But money may not necessarily have been the real motive. I gather he wasn't on very good terms with his father.'

'It seems that Sidney wasn't a very nice person,' I said cautiously, 'but I believe you know that. I don't think he treated David very well.'

'I see.'

'Now we know what sort of person Sidney really was,' I went on, 'it may be that there were other people who might have had reasons for disliking him.'

'Do you know of anyone else?' Roger asked.

'Well, no,' I said, 'but that doesn't mean there aren't any. After all, the business with Bill Goddard's brother has only just come to light.'

'That's true. Keep your ears open and let me know if you hear anything.'

'Yes, of course.'

Roger leaned forward. 'Sheila, Sidney Middleton may not, as you say, have been a very nice person, better off dead, perhaps. But the fact remains that he was murdered and whatever we may think about the ins and outs of the affair, taking a life is against the law and it is, in the last resort, wrong. That's why I have to investigate his death and that is why I need all the information I can get, no matter what it is and who may be hurt by it.' He looked at his watch. 'Is that the time? I must be going. Give my love to Thea and Michael. Take care of yourself.'

I sat quite still for a while, taking in the force of Roger's reproof, since reproof it was, however courteously delivered, and of course, I admitted to myself, he was right. We can't go taking the law into our own hands however terrible the provocation. It is not for us to balance one life against another, however much we may feel our reasons are right and just.

For the rest of the day I was restless and couldn't settle properly to anything. I kept thinking about what Roger had said and trying to decide if I should tell him everything I knew about Brian and David. Should I tell him, too, about Bill Goddard's solitary walks when he could so easily have removed that inspection plate? My conscience said I should but I still felt in my heart that it would be some sort of betrayal.

'How much easier it would have been if Sidney had been as nice as we always thought he was,' I said to Foss as he settled beside me on the sofa while I flicked back and forth between the television channels trying to find something to take my mind off the problem. 'Then there would have been no doubt at all about wanting his killer caught. I still can't believe how easily he deceived us all and for so long.'

Foss, irritated by my restlessness, jumped down from the sofa and made his way into the kitchen, loudly demanding his supper, closely followed by Tris with a similar object in mind. I put down their saucers and decided I might as well go to bed myself. It really hadn't been a very satisfactory day and to soothe myself I picked up the copy of *Sense and Sensibility* that lay on my bedside table and, opening it at random (as one can with well-loved books), I began to read.

"'I have frequently detected myself in such kind of mistakes,' said Elinor, 'in a total misapprehension of character in some point or other ... and I can hardly tell why or in what the deception originated. Sometimes one is guided by what they say of themselves, and very frequently by what other people say of them, without giving oneself time to deliberate and judge.'"

I laid down the book with a smile and thought once again how Jane Austen never fails one. Then I picked it up again and lost myself gratefully in the doings of the family at Barton Cottage.

16

The next day I felt more cheerful. There was a hint of Spring in the air. A patch of snowdrops by the stream had been transformed overnight from anonymous green spikes into delicate bells of white and, as I drove into Taviscombe after lunch, I saw with pleasure that some of the early municipal daffodils were in bloom on the grass verges and traffic islands. After my conversation with Roger I felt a bit guilty that I hadn't told him everything I knew, so I thought I'd go and visit Bill Goddard and try to decide once and for all whether he might have had anything to do with Sidney Middleton's death. When I got there, though, no one was in. I rang the bell several times and was just about to give up and go home when a voice behind me said,

'Did you want Bill and Betty? They've gone to the doctor's.' I turned round and saw Myra Norton. 'Oh it's you, Mrs Malory, I'm so sorry I didn't recognise you from behind. No, like I said, they've gone to the doctor's – just a check-up for Bill – but they won't be long. Would you like to come in and have a cup of tea with me while you wait?'

'That's very kind of you,' I said, 'but I don't want to put you to any trouble...'

'Oh, it's no trouble,' she said heartily, 'Jim's out and I'll be glad of the company.'

I followed her up the path and into the bungalow. 'That's really kind of you,' I said. 'I just wondered how Bill is – I brought him a few gardening magazines.'

'Oh he'll like those, he's a great one for his garden. Not that there's much you can do at this time of the year, really dismal it's been. Still, it's nice and bright today. Do come and sit down in the lounge while I put the kettle on. Now do make yourself at home, I won't be a minute.'

When she had gone I looked about me. Apart from a fiercely patterned carpet the predominant shade was beige – furniture, curtains, even the cushions. There was a light-wood sideboard and a fitment against one of the walls holding a few books and many small ornaments, and a lot of house plants were standing on a multiplicity of occasional tables. There were no pictures but there were several photographs on the sideboard. One was the Nortons' wedding photograph – the young Myra Norton, beaming happily in white satin and orange blossom with an enormous bouquet of lilies and Jim Norton, acutely uncomfortable in a tailcoat and striped trousers. Another was of a young girl, about 10 or 11, in school uniform, blazer, white shirt and striped tie, fair-haired with a pleasant though not especially pretty face. The third was of a young man wearing a gown and mortar board, holding some sort of rolled up certificate. He had dark hair and an anxious expression. I was struck by the stiff posed formality of all three photographs and wondered who the two young people were. Then it struck me that they might be the young Jim and Myra Norton – the clothes, after all, were timeless, and it seemed rather touching that they should wish to display only these images of their former selves.

'There we are then.' She was back in the room putting down a tray of tea things on yet another small table. 'How do you like it? Weak, strong or just as it comes? Milk and sugar?'

'Strong please, with just a little milk and no sugar.'

To her evident disappointment I declined

in turn a chocolate biscuit, a piece of shortbread and a lemon slice but I accepted the tea gratefully.

'That's lovely,' I said, 'just how I like it.'

As I drank my tea I surreptitiously compared the photograph of the girl with the person before me and decided there was a strong possibility that they were indeed one and the same person.

'No, Bill's made a very good recovery,' she was saying. 'Poor soul, he was really very ill, but the doctor made him have a chest X-ray, well, you can't be too careful, can you, and so they've gone in today to get the result. Betty was quite worried, but I said, "No, mark my words, it'll be all right. If there'd been anything wrong they'd have rung you straight away". Well, they do, don't they?'

'I'm sure you're right. He did seem much better when I saw him last and it's been quite a mild Winter on the whole.'

'Oh yes, we've been very lucky and these bungalows are very easy to keep warm. Good insulation, Jim says, and the central heating is wonderful. I have to turn it right down sometimes it's so warm. Mind you, central heating's all very well, but I do miss having a fireplace – no mantelpiece to put things on and nothing that you can call a *focus* to the room.'

'It's all very cosy,' I said, 'and your plants seem to thrive, they're really splendid.'

'Oh, I've always had a knack with house-plants. Jim says I've got green fingers. Now he's a marvel with electrical things. He's at Brunswick Lodge right now, fixing something or other.'

'He's been wonderful,' I said. 'We're so grateful to him for all that he does there.'

She laughed. 'It's a blessing really, him having an interest like that. He wouldn't know what to do with himself if he didn't have something to keep him busy. Now, are you sure you won't have a lemon slice? No? Another cup of tea then?'

'No, really, I won't thanks. Actually, I think I'd better be going. I'll call on Bill and Betty some other time.'

'No, don't do that. They'll be here in a minute, I'm sure. Betty said they'd be coming straight back. Just between ourselves I think she's still worried about Bill, not just his chest, but that business with his brother, *you* know. It upset him terribly, well it would, wouldn't it? He used to go off on his own, sometimes late at night. I've seen him come back in the small hours – I don't sleep very well, old age I suppose – and I often get up and make myself a hot drink and when I heard the gate go I looked through the window and there he was. It gave me quite a turn seeing him at that time of night.'

'I can see that would be worrying. Poor Betty.'

'Well, we must hope he's on the mend now, though they do say that any sort of *mental* problem takes much longer to put right.'

'Oh I don't think it's as bad as that.'

'Well perhaps not...' She broke off and went to the window. 'That's them coming back now.'

'Right. I'll just give them a moment to get in,' I said, 'and then I'll be off. Thank you so much for the tea, it was very kind of you.'

'It's always nice to have a chat. Do drop in any time.'

Bill and Betty seemed pleased to see me. My arrival was the signal for Betty to put the kettle on, although I protested that I'd just had a cup of tea with Mrs Norton.

'Oh, I'm sure you can manage another one, dear. And, after sitting about in that waiting room so long, I'm absolutely gasping!' she said as she bustled off into the kitchen.

'You know Betty with her cups of tea,' Bill laughed.

'It's lovely to see you looking like your old self again,' I said. 'Obviously that break in Bournemouth did you a lot of good.'

'Oh yes, Susan and Trevor really went out of their way to make us welcome and it was a good chance to see the grandchildren.'

'That was nice.'

'But it wasn't just that,' Bill said. 'Before we went David Middleton came to see me. You can imagine, he was the last person I expected to see. He said he had to come, said he wanted to apologise. I couldn't think what to make of it – that man's son! And I never really had much time for young David the few times I met him. But then he explained, he came right out and told me all sorts about his father and the way he and his mother had been treated all those years. I couldn't hardly believe it!'

'I'm pretty sure it's true,' I said. 'He's spoken to me about it too and so did – so did someone else, who's suffered almost as much as David. It's very obvious that Sidney Middleton was a really horrible man. That awful thing he did in the war seems to have been part and parcel of the same thing. He was just – well, *horrible!*'

Bill nodded. 'I was really impressed with the way young David didn't try to make any excuses. He said he should have let people know somehow what his father was really like. But then, the things he told me, things I couldn't repeat, about what he and his mother had to go through – well, it doesn't bear thinking about.'

'I know. David told me a little about their life together and, like you, I found it dreadfully upsetting.'

'He said he felt guilty, like he was responsible for what that man had done because he'd never said anything. But I told him that was nonsense, especially when he'd suffered more than anyone!'

'I know.'

Bill settled back more comfortably in his chair. 'After he'd said all that we had a nice chat and he asked all sorts of questions about Frank and what I'd done in the war. He seemed really interested and said could he bring one of his boys round one day because he was doing some project at school about the war and he'd like him to hear what I could tell him.'

'That would be really nice,' I said.

'Yes, I'd like to think of some of the young people of today knowing what it was really like back then.'

'Oh, I do agree. I know there are books and all those television programmes, but it's not the same as actually talking to someone who was actually *there*.'

Betty came in with the tea tray and to please her I had a piece of date and walnut cake as well as the tea.

'Did Bill tell you about David Middleton?' she asked.

'Yes, he did.'

'You could have knocked me down with a feather when I saw who it was on the doorstep. But he was really nice. He and Bill had a proper old talk, didn't you, Bill, and the things he told him – well, I couldn't believe there was so much wickedness in the world! That man had a lot to answer for.'

'He certainly did,' I said. 'Though I suppose he did pay for it in the end.'

'Dying like that, all peaceful-like, was too good for him,' Betty said vigorously. 'He should have suffered like he made others suffer.'

'Well, he's gone now,' Bill said, 'and that's that. Mind you, when it first happened, when I heard about Frank and the others, I really saw red. I wanted to go round there and have it out with him, I think I told you.

To be honest, Sheila, I wanted to go round there and wring his neck!'

'That's very understandable,' I said.

'I think I was a bit mad then, I could have done anything. I went out walking, for hours sometimes, well, Betty will tell you. Really worried, she was. Just to try and walk it all off. Once I even went as far as his lane, but then I turned back. You see, whatever I did to him, it wouldn't bring Frank back, and it would bring me down to his level, if you see what I mean.'

'You're absolutely right,' I said.

'So I won't say I'm sorry he's dead. It seems to me that there's a lot of people better off now he's gone – people who'd be glad to shake the hand of whoever it was who did it!'

'Oh Bill,' Betty protested, 'you oughtn't to talk like that. Whatever will Sheila think!'

'I agree with Bill,' I said. 'The world's a much better place without him.'

'So that seems to be that,' I said to Thea. 'In spite of the long walks at night and no alibi, I'm absolutely sure that Bill had nothing to do with Stanley Middleton's death. It's not just that he's an old friend, well, in a way it's *because* he is, that I'm positive that what he

239

told me was the truth. And, although he'd been almost as far as Lamb's Cottage, when the actual moment came he'd turned back. That's the Bill Goddard I've known all my life, that's what he would do.'

'I'm sure you're right,' Thea said, 'but after all you were equally sure that Sidney Middleton was a nice chap and you'd known him all your life too.'

'Oh dear,' I said, 'when you put it like that. But I've seen how Bill is with other people, how genuine he is. Anyway,' I finished triumphantly, 'there's Betty as well. There's no way Betty would marry someone who wasn't thoroughly nice and good!'

'That's true,' Thea agreed. 'But if he didn't do it, who's left?'

'Well, there's David, of course, and Brian. Goodness knows both of them had reason enough to want their father dead.'

'And they've neither of them got an alibi?'

'Apparently not.'

'But there's no proof that either of them did it?'

'As far as I can see there's no proof that anyone did it.'

'Perhaps it will be one of those cases that are never solved,' Thea said. 'That would surely be the best thing.'

'But as Roger said,' I replied, 'it's against the law, so I don't see him giving up. It's just that it seems so hard when they've both of them suffered so much. Isn't there something called justifiable homicide, or is that only in American movies?'

'The law is a bit more complicated than that,' Thea said. 'But are Brian and David the only two people that would have a motive? Surely there must be others, people in London perhaps, he's injured in some way?'

'All his business life was in London, and if that was as foul as his private life then I've no doubt he wrecked a lot of people's lives, so Roger should certainly do some investigating there.'

'Well, there you are, then.'

'Mm. I don't think it's as easy as that. I mean, people from London hanging around would stick out like a sore thumb – you know what the country's like, anything or anyone out of the ordinary is immediately spotted! Besides, how would they know about the wood-burning stove and the inspection plate? No, much as I would like it to be someone we don't know, I don't see how it can be.'

'I suppose not,' Thea agreed regretfully.

'Actually,' I said, after a moment, 'I've been wondering *why* we always thought Sidney was such a splendid person.'

'What do you mean?'

'He was always charming when he met you,' I said, 'polite and courteous, like most men of his generation. He always seemed interested in what you were doing. He was a good listener.'

'He was very generous,' Thea said. 'People always went to him first for donations to things.'

'Yes, he always gave generously to charities, but have you ever heard of him doing anything generous to a *person?*'

'Well, no, but one wouldn't necessarily...'

'And did he have any friends – I mean real friends?'

'There were Dick and Marjorie in the village.'

'Yes, they used to give him lifts and things when he couldn't drive any more, but that was because they were sorry for him when they thought David was being beastly to him. And the old army people, they looked up to him, admired him for "having no side" as they used to say, but that was all.'

'Your parents liked him,' Thea said. 'Well, you did too.'

'I know, that's what I'm trying to work out. He was of my parents' generation, they appeared to like him, I'd known him all my life, so I took it for granted that he was a nice person. True, he wasn't a close friend of the family, we simply moved in the same circles. My father always saw the best in people so it's not surprising that he accepted Sidney, but my mother was pretty sharp, she usually spotted when something wasn't right. How could she have missed it?'

'But he'd presented that face to the world all his life,' Thea said. 'The same face to everyone, always. There was no one to contradict him – his wife, David, they were too frightened even to hint that there might be something wrong. I daresay if you say something loud enough and long enough, like, "I am a good and charming person", people will believe you. Why wouldn't they?'

'You're probably right,' I said. 'I suppose I just resent having been fooled.'

'Who wouldn't? Anyway, will you stay to lunch? It'll only be soup and cheese, if that's all right.'

'That'll be lovely.'

Alice came into the room clutching a toy elephant in one hand and a video in the other.

'Row the boat!' she demanded, holding out the video.

Thea groaned. 'Oh, darling, do you really want it again?' She turned to me. 'It's that nursery rhyme video she adores. But if I have to hear row the boat and the wheels on the wretched bus *one* more time I think I'll go crazy!'

'Wretched bus, wretched bus,' Alice chanted happily, thrusting the video into her hand.

Thea passed it over to me. 'Gran will watch it with you,' she said, 'while I get lunch. After all,' she added with a sweet smile in my direction, 'that's what Grans are for.'

17

A few days later I ran into Rosemary in the greengrocer's.

'Hello,' I said, 'whatever's the matter? You look positively harassed.'

'I *feel* harassed. Mother's not been very well, just a chill, but she's had to stay in bed for a few days and you know how she hates that!'

'Oh dear.'

'And all she can bear to eat, so she says, is halibut and avocado pear.'

'Together!'

'No, separately. Oh, and charantais melon. I've got the melon but halibut's out of the question and all the avocados are rock hard.' She picked one up and prodded it. 'There, just feel that! And they're all the same.'

'I believe it helps to soften them if you put them in a paper bag with a ripe banana, but I suppose it would take too long.'

'Much too long,' Rosemary said gloomily. 'Jilly said something about putting them in the microwave, but if I did that I'd probably end up with a squidgy mess.'

'Probably,' I agreed. 'I expect she's just bored. Would it help if I went to see her?'

'Oh, would you? I know she'd like that.'

'Of course. I'll ring Elsie when I get home to see when's a good time.'

Mrs Dudley was in bed propped up on a bank of pillows, white pillows, of course (since she held coloured bed linen to be vulgar) with white embroidery, something I hadn't seen for many years and which took me back to the time when my mother and I would spend a whole morning 'turning out' the linen cupboard. She was wearing a high-necked Viyella nightdress and a pale blue knitted bed-jacket and her hair was as impeccable as ever. In other words, Mrs Dudley was herself as always and nothing, not even illness, was allowed to alter her imposing image. She gave me a fleeting smile as I handed her the pot of African violets I had brought.

'Thank you Sheila, they are delightful. Such a pity one can't get real parma violets nowadays. I remember when I was a young girl, one always wore a bunch pinned to one's fur coat.'

I didn't mention that fur coats were now

as obsolete as parma violets. She put the pot down on her bedside table and motioned me to a chair placed near the bed.

'Now then, what news?' she asked.

I gave her the items of gossip about mutual acquaintances that I had carefully garnered to prepare me for this visit, but when I had run out of material, as it were, Mrs Dudley, although pleased with the quality of the information, seemed disappointed at its quantity. She allowed a silence to fall, always, with her, a sign of disapproval, so I cast about for some other topic that might interest her.

'What was Sidney Middleton like as a young man?' I asked.

She became animated again. 'Ambitious, of course,' she said, 'and ruthless, but with that sort of superficial charm that fools so many people.' Here she gave me a beady-eyed look that indicated that she included me in that category. 'Completely amoral in every way, no principles and spiteful.'

'Spiteful?'

'Oh yes – a sort of envy. He couldn't bear anyone to have anything he wanted, or thought he wanted, and he would go to any lengths to harm anyone who did. As I said, spiteful.'

'What sort of lengths?' I asked.

She thought for a minute and then said, 'Joseph Middleton, his cousin.'

'I never knew he had a cousin. He never mentioned one.'

'Well, he wouldn't, he couldn't stand him. Just before the war Joseph married someone Sidney Middleton had his eye on. Cynthia Meadows, a handsome girl, everyone said, though I could never see it myself, with her own money (from her grandmother I believe), and ambitious, as ambitious as Sidney. He proposed but she turned him down. She probably saw through him just as I did, she was no fool.'

'Good for her,' I said.

Mrs Dudley gave me a grim smile. 'Unfortunately she married Joseph instead. One can see why. He was a better catch (he had his own business, engineering of some sort) and was obviously going to succeed in life. Also he was very good-looking, though that is hardly a sound basis for a successful married life – on the contrary, in most cases.'

'So what happened?'

'The war came and both Sidney and Joseph were called up. Sidney went into the Army, and we all know what happened *there*, and Joseph was in the Navy. He had some sort of secret job, something to do with developing new weapons, because of his engineering experience, I suppose. He wasn't allowed to talk about it during the war, of course, but afterwards, when the details came out, it all seemed quite glamorous.' She gave a scornful smile. 'People are influenced by such things. Look how dreadful life is today!'

'I know.'

'As you can imagine,' she continued, 'with this old rivalry between them, Sidney was very jealous indeed. He'd married poor little Joan by then so he had at least as much money as Joseph, but he didn't have Joseph's – what is that people say now? – charisma!' She brought out the word triumphantly. 'Ridiculous expression! But it made Sidney Middleton furious.'

'So what did he do?'

'There wasn't much he could do but watch and wait. Joseph became more and more successful in business, a millionaire, I believe, and that *meant* something in those days, not like nowadays with every Tom, Dick and Harry winning this appalling lottery thing. They had three children and a very fine house, an old manor house somewhere in the Blackdown Hills. I remember seeing pictures of it in *Country Life*. Joseph was absolutely obsessed by this house, spent a fortune on it I believe, *not* a very wise thing to do as it turned out.'

'Really?'

'He was stupid in other ways, too,' Mrs Dudley went on. 'He had an affair with this young woman, someone who worked for him, quite a common girl but men are so silly about a pretty face. Mind you, I wasn't at all surprised when it all came out. Cynthia Middleton was a difficult woman to live with, very domineering, always insisted on her own way in everything, something I have absolutely no patience with. I always feel that there must be give and take in this life, don't you agree?'

Fortunately the question was rhetorical so I was not required to do more than nod, suppressing any doubts I might have had about the accuracy of Mrs Dudley's feelings in this matter.

'It was obviously only a matter of time before he broke out in this way and a sensible woman would have known how to ignore it. But Cynthia Middleton was the sort of person who couldn't bear to think she wasn't in control of the situation. Her pride was hurt, of course, but she behaved very foolishly. If she had hushed it up no one would have known anything about it, but she made a great fuss – solicitors, a divorce, both of them dragged through the courts. This was some years ago, of course, when divorce was considered a great disgrace. So different now when young people who actually do get married (and not many of them do that!) think nothing of divorcing after the first little disagreement!'

She looked at me sharply and I said, 'Oh, absolutely.'

'He lost practically everything. Naturally she had the very best lawyer. The business had to be sold and the house – there was no way he could buy her out. It broke his heart losing that house. I do believe he minded losing that more than he minded losing the children. Anyway, she went to Canada soon after and took the children with her and he never saw them again from that day to this.'

'How awful. What happened to him?'

'Oh, he went to pieces. He married the girl after the divorce came through, but it wasn't a success. She left him. He lost a lot of money, you see, trying to start up a business again. The last I heard, he was living in a tiny little flat in Taunton. I don't know *what* he lives on – I suppose he has an old age pension.'

'He must be quite old now. Was he the same age as Sidney?'

'A little younger, but I believe still quite active.'

'I see.' I thought for a moment and then I said, 'But what has this to do with Sidney?'

Mrs Dudley leaned forward from her bank of pillows and said confidentially, 'Well, who do you think it was who told Cynthia Middleton about her husband's affair?'

'You mean...?'

'Exactly. When he found out about it – and I don't suppose *that* was too difficult, since Joseph Middleton was not exactly the soul of discretion – Sidney went straight round to Cynthia, oh so sympathetic, but egging her on all the time to divorce Joseph.'

'How awful.'

'Well, Joseph Middleton was a fool, I have no patience with him, but I do believe if it hadn't been for Sidney they might just have patched things up. But he kept on telling Cynthia how badly she'd been treated, how she owed it to herself to take a stand, that sort of thing.'

'I see.'

'It was quite a scandal at the time,' Mrs Dudley said with some satisfaction. She picked up the small handbell from the table

252

beside her bed and rang vigorously. 'Time for my brandy. Dr Macdonald says I must have a little brandy twice a day to keep my strength up. Can I offer you anything, Sheila, a glass of sherry, perhaps? I think it is near enough lunchtime for that to be suitable.'

I shook my head. 'No thank you. I really ought to be going. I promised to look after Alice this afternoon while Thea goes to the dentist.'

'It was good of you to call,' Mrs Dudley said graciously. 'While you are up, would you mind passing me the paper? It's on the chair by the window.'

I went over and picked up the *Daily Telegraph* ('*The Times* is *not* what it was'), folded back at the obituaries page. I put it down beside her and kissed her powdered cheek.

'Take care of yourself,' I said, 'and get well soon.'

'So you see,' I said to Thea while we were having lunch, 'there's yet another person who had a motive for killing Sidney.

'But this cousin must be pretty ancient by now,' Thea said doubtfully.

'Mrs Dudley said he was quite active.'

'Still...'

'Well, even if it wasn't him,' I persisted, 'it just shows that there are all sorts of people who had very good reasons to wish he was dead.'

'You're just pleased to have found someone with a motive that you don't actually know.'

'Well, there is that, but the general principle stands, you must agree.'

'Of course I agree, but you must remember – oh, darling, *don't* do that!'

Alice, annoyed at being ignored, had decided to attract our attention by pouring her mug of Ribena partly over the remains of her mashed potatoes and partly over the tablecloth. In the general confusion of clearing up the mess and getting Thea off for her appointment, I never did get to hear what it was she thought I should remember.

Nevertheless, in spite of what Thea had said, I just couldn't help mentioning it to Roger when I saw him, dog-walking as I was, on the beach.

'It does show,' I said, when I had reported the gist of Mrs Dudley's story, 'that there may be masses of people with motives for killing Sidney Middleton.'

Roger smiled. 'Why is it,' he enquired,

'that whenever *I* have a conversation with my grandmother-in-law, all I get is a lecture on how badly we're bringing up Delia and Alex?'

'But seriously, Roger...'

'Seriously, I will, of course, pursue the lead you have kindly given me, though, I must say, I don't think it's going to lead anywhere in particular.'

'But there may very well be people elsewhere. Have you checked his business activities in London?' I persisted.

'Yes, we've been into all that and, although he was considered to be a shrewd operator in his day, sometimes a bit borderline, there's no evidence that he gave anyone cause to want to actually murder him.'

'Oh,' I said, deflated. 'So you still think it was someone here, someone local?'

'That does seem to be the most likely option. The people down here had the strongest reason for wanting him dead.'

'But why should whoever it is have waited till now, why not have killed him ages ago?'

'Well, Bill Goddard, for example, only found out recently about that letter.'

'Oh *no*,' I said vehemently, 'I know it can't be Bill!'

Roger shook his head. 'You *believe* he

couldn't have done it because you know and like him, but you don't actually *know*.'

'That's nonsense,' I said impatiently.

'And Brian Thorpe,' Roger continued. 'He may have had some special reason for wanting the cottage and the money Middleton left him at this particular time.'

'But *you* don't know that.'

'No, I don't. There's no evidence for any of this, it's all supposition and, on that basis, there's no way I can put together a case against any of the suspects that would stand up in court.'

'I see.'

'I'm sorry Sheila, but you do see I must keep an open mind and evaluate the facts – I repeat, the facts – as I see them.'

'Yes, of course. I'm sorry, Roger, for being so tiresome!'

'You shouldn't get yourself so involved in other people's lives,' Roger said, 'but then I don't suppose you'll ever stop doing that.'

Tris, who'd been investigating some unidentified sea creature on the edge of a rockpool, began to dig vigorously, showering us with sand.

'Oh dear,' I said, 'I'd better take him back before he gets covered in wet sand. He *will* shake himself all over the inside of the car and it's the very devil to clear up. Give my love to Jilly and the children.'

Michael called that evening, to return a lamp he'd repaired for me, and I told him what I'd learnt from Mrs Dudley.

'Joe Middleton,' Michael said. 'Yes I know him. Nice chap, made a great success of that antiques business.'

'Antiques?'

'He owns that place in Taunton, the something-or-other Gallery just off the Precinct.'

'The Oriental Gallery. But that's very grand!'

'Yes, well, he's some kind of expert in Oriental stuff, people come from all over to consult him. He's been on the telly on some of those antique programmes you're always watching. I'm surprised you haven't seen him.'

'*That* Joe Middleton, yes, of course I've seen him, but I never made the connection. How do you know him?'

'Oh, we've acted for him a couple of times. He was a friend of Edward's parents, so he knows him quite well.'

'I see. But how did he get into antiques? I mean, after losing his business and all that. It seems like such a massive change of direction.'

'Apparently he'd always been interested in that sort of thing, but he'd never had the time to do more than dabble. When he went through that bad patch, he said, he decided to give it a go. He read up all he could and had a couple of lucky finds at auctions and so forth and it just sort of snowballed from there.'

'How extraordinary. Do you know anything about his private life?'

'He married a while back, a nice woman, used to be some sort of curator at the Indian Institute in Oxford, that's how they met. She was a widow with a couple of children. They're grown-up now, of course, but he seems devoted to them.'

'Well! I do hope Sidney knew all this, he'd have been absolutely *furious*. Especially about being on television. After all, that is the final accolade nowadays, isn't it?'

'It is a success story, certainly.'

'A happy ending, in fact.'

'You could say that. Is that the time? I'd better be going, Thea will have supper ready.'

'Yes, of course. Bless you for mending the lamp. It's always been a favourite of mine.'

As I put on the potatoes for my own supper, my main feeling was of astonishment that, in all the years I'd known her, Mrs Dudley's information was incomplete. Of course I could never tell her so and doubtless the local intelligence service would bring her up to date, but still it was a shock to find that she was not, as we had all thought, infallible. My instinctive feeling of triumph gave way, however, to one of sadness. I didn't want to think about it, but I had to recognise the fact that Mrs Dudley, the last authority figure for my generation, was getting old and one day would no longer be with us.

18

I felt a bit foolish, having presented Joe Middleton to Roger as a possible new suspect when obviously he wasn't, so I didn't get in touch with him right away to correct the supposition. In any case I was trying to nerve myself to finish a review which was proving tiresome. I'd just switched on the computer and was trying to marshal my thoughts about yet another book on the influence of the industrial revolution on the Victorian novel, with special reference to the works of the women writers of that period, when the bell rang. It was Brian.

'I've got the wood for those shelves,' he said as he came into the room. 'Would this be a good time? Oh dear, no it isn't. I'm sorry, you were working. I'll come back another day.'

'No,' I said, closing down the computer. 'I'm glad of an excuse to stop. You carry on. Would you like a cup of tea?'

'A bit later, perhaps. I'll just bring the wood in and get started.'

'That's fine. I'll be in the kitchen if you want anything.'

Out in the kitchen a bowl of Seville oranges mutely reproached me. Making marmalade was another thing I'd been putting off. Deciding that if I couldn't do one task I'd better do the other, I got out the chopping board and a knife and started preparing the oranges. Soon the whole kitchen, my whole universe indeed, was filled with the smell of them and as I stood patiently stirring the delicious mixture in the old preserving pan that had belonged to my mother, I tried to remember when I'd first been entrusted with this annual task. It was, I decided, when I was still at Oxford, at the end of one Christmas vacation and the thought of cutting up oranges was more inviting than sitting in my room trying to make sense of *Beowulf*. I suddenly had a vivid sense of just how long ago that time was and, like my thoughts about Mrs Dudley, I had a painful reminder of my own, and others', mortality.

The marmalade had set quite nicely and I was just filling the warmed jars when there was a tap on the door and Brian came in.

'Just to say I've finished putting up the shelves,' he said, 'and I've primed them. I'll come and finish the painting another day.'

'Oh, that's splendid. Just let me finish this and I'll make us a cup of tea.'

'It all smells very good,' he said.

'You must have a pot, if you'd like one.' I put the waxed disc on the last jar. 'I'll let these cool down while I put the kettle on. Do go into the sitting-room. The smell of oranges is nice for a bit but it does get rather overpowering!'

While we were drinking our tea I asked about his mother.

'I told you, didn't I, that David – he asked me to call him David – said he'd come back and have a proper talk. Well, he did. Mother was really pleased to see him. I couldn't believe it; she wasn't nervous at all. She'd even made some little cakes specially when she knew he was coming. It was like a miracle. When she went to have her rest he told me about his own mother, all that she'd gone through, and how he'd had to learn how to look out for her and try and comfort her when things were really bad, even though he'd been having a bad time himself. So then, it sort of made sense, the way Mother trusted him.'

'Yes, I can see that.'

'The things he told me about his own life

don't bear thinking about. I could hardly believe some of them, but I'm sure they were true.' He stopped suddenly. 'I shouldn't be saying all this – he told me in confidence...'

'It's all right,' I said, 'I know all about it. David told me himself.'

Brian looked relieved. 'That's all right, then.' He took one of the biscuits I offered. 'Thanks. Like I told you before, it's really good to be able to talk to somebody about it. I mean, it's all so strange, lots of people simply wouldn't believe it.'

'Oh, I believe it all right,' I said. 'The more I learn about Sidney Middleton ... well!'

'What David said was so frightening was the way he gradually found himself turning into the person his father said he was. That was really weird.'

'It can happen,' I said. 'But I'm so glad you've been able to talk to each other about things.'

'It's made a real difference,' Brian said earnestly. 'I sort of feel a weight's been lifted off my shoulders.'

'That's wonderful.'

'Of course,' he continued, 'there's still the police.'

'I gather you neither of you have an alibi?'

'Well...' he hesitated.

'Yes?'

'I didn't tell the police exactly where I was.'

'What do you mean?' I asked anxiously. 'Where were you that night?'

He hesitated, then he said, 'I was most of the night in the Casualty department in Musgrove hospital.'

'In Casualty!'

'Yes. It's a long story...'

'Whatever happened, and why on earth didn't you tell the police?'

He shrugged. 'It's all a bit complicated. You see, Margaret rang me that evening. Mark had been larking about and he'd fallen quite heavily and she thought his arm was broken. So I said she must get him to hospital but she said she couldn't because Carol, that's the little girl, was ill in bed with a bad ear infection. She'd got a temperature and was really ill so Margaret couldn't leave her or take her to the hospital too.'

'No, of course not.'

'She begged me to take Mark to Casualty – he knows me and he'd go with me all right. But she knew how difficult it is. Mother can't bear being left alone at night. She gets really frightened and upset if I'm not there. Well, I looked in on Mother and

264

she was sleeping really soundly because she'd taken some of her tablets to make her sleep, so I thought I'd risk it. I had to, Margaret sounded so desperate. She's got no family, you see, and her neighbours are an old couple who wouldn't be much help.'

'Yes, I can see that.'

'So I got the van out and collected Mark. He was really miserable, poor little chap. But when we got to the hospital they had an emergency and we had to wait for hours before we were seen and then there was all the business about X-rays – it was broken – and having the plaster put on and so forth, so by the time we'd finished it was almost daylight!'

'How dreadful.'

'I took him back and just managed to get home before Mother woke up, so it was all right in the end.'

'But that's a perfectly good alibi,' I said. 'Why on earth didn't you tell the police that that's where you were? I mean, it's something they could easily check on.'

'The trouble is,' Brian said slowly, 'that when that Inspector came Mother was upset, like you'd expect having a strange man calling, so she went out of the room.'

'So?'

'But I knew she'd be listening outside the door. That's the way she is, nervous and suspicious of everyone. So I knew she'd hear what I said. Well, the fact is, I didn't want her to know that I'd been out that night and left her there all alone.'

'Yes, I can see that. But,' I continued, 'why didn't you go and call at the police station and tell them there?'

He was silent for a moment. 'I was going to, but I kept putting it off, you know, like you do, and then David came and we talked and he said *he* hadn't got an alibi, so I thought if I told the police where I was then it would all be on David. He'd be the only suspect they had left. I thought if there were two of us, then maybe it would confuse things...' His voice trailed away. 'I didn't care if he *had* killed the old bastard,' he went on, 'he'd had every reason to. I wish I'd done it myself years ago!'

'I'm sure you do,' I said, 'but please don't go around saying that, even if you do have a perfectly good alibi. But seriously, though, you must tell the police. I'm sure it won't affect the way they regard David. Anyway, there's absolutely no evidence against him.'

'Are you sure?'

'If there had been they would have

questioned him again.' He still looked doubtful, so I went on, 'I know you want to help David in any way you can, but you must tell the police where you were. I'm sure that's what he'd want you to do.'

'Well, if you think so.'

'I do.'

'All right, I will then. But, if I didn't kill him and David didn't – and I'm pretty sure he didn't – then who did?'

'I really don't know, and, as far as I can tell, the police have no idea either. I think we must all get on with our lives and leave it to them.'

When Brian had gone I finished off the marmalade and, as I put it away in the larder, I felt a great sense of relief that he did have an alibi. I hadn't, in the beginning, believed he'd killed Sidney Middleton because he seemed too quiet and gentle a person. But, as I learned more about his life and what he and his mother had been through, I'd certainly had doubts. His motive would have been very strong. So it was good to know that my first impression of him had been right. But, if Brian was no longer a suspect, then that only left David. He too had a motive, even stronger than Brian's, but, having discovered the 'new'

David, I was very reluctant to think of him as a murderer.

Foss, attracted by my presence in the kitchen, emerged from the study, where he'd been sleeping on a pile of copies of *The Journal of the Jane Austen Society*, and wound round my legs, loudly demanding food. When he'd rejected the tinned food I offered him and I'd warmed up the remains of his fish in the microwave, it was time to go and meet Anthea at Brunswick Lodge to arrange about the collection of things for the next jumble sale, so I had other things to think about.

'I'm leaving the books to you,' Anthea said, 'because you know about such things. Paperbacks always go well and Mary Perry is moving house. She's going into one of those bungalows in Regents Close, poky little places, very little space, so she's having to throw out a lot of things. She says she's got a couple of boxes of books she wants to get rid of, so I said you'd go round there today and collect them. Oh, and while you're there, she said she had some curtains that are the wrong size for the new windows, so you might see what they're like and if they'd be any use to us.'

I refrained from telling Anthea that my

literary activities did not automatically qualify me for heaving boxes of books about, but meekly took my instructions.

'Then,' Anthea went on, 'if you and Rosemary can come in next week and sort through the clothes... Yes, I know it's a nuisance but I don't want to ask Edith Spencer again. Last time she did it, she picked out a lot of the really good stuff for herself, and that's really not on!'

I knew better than to interrupt Anthea when she was in full flow so I merely nodded.

'Oh, and something's the matter with the light switches in the Committee Room. The whole place was plunged into darkness last Wednesday. We'd better get Jim Norton to come and see to it. I did try to phone him yesterday but there was no reply. If you happen to be going in that direction you could call in and ask him.'

Since that was tantamount to a command, I didn't say that the Norton's house was in a totally different direction from Mary Perry's, but nodded again and made my escape before Anthea could find any other task for me to do.

It had begun to rain, not heavily but per-sistently, a cold miserable rain and I didn't feel much like driving round Taviscombe collecting jumble and delivering messages. Even returning to my tiresome review seemed preferable. Still, I got into the car and drove to Mary Perry's. After some time and several cups of tea I finally made my escape. Mary is a good soul and I'm very fond of her but she is the sort of person who hates to be alone and her passion for company (any old company) means that it's very difficult to get away. One makes many false starts, but she always remembers one more thing she has to tell you and there you are, standing uncomfortably with one hand on the doorknob unable to get away until she's wrung the last drop, as it were, from your visit. I loaded the boxes of books and a motley collection of curtains (I didn't stop to see if they were 'any use' or not) into the boot and quickly drove away.

I couldn't make anyone hear at the Norton's house and I decided to go back and telephone later from the comfort of my own home. Just as I got to the gate the door of the Goddards' bungalow next door was opened and Betty put her head out.

'Hello, Sheila,' she called. 'I thought it was you standing there. They're out all day. Was it anything important?'

'No, it's just a message for Jim Norton from Anthea about Brunswick Lodge. I can easily phone him later.'

'Now you're here, do come in and have a word with Bill, he'd love to see you.'

I followed her into the sitting-room, where I found Bill sitting watching a quiz show on television.

'Don't switch off on my account,' I said, as he reached for the remote control.

'No, it's all rubbish, anyway,' he said, 'just something to watch.'

'So how are you keeping?' I asked. 'No more bronchitis, I hope.'

'No, he's been really fit since we got back from Bournemouth,' Betty said, 'haven't you, love?'

'Oh, I'm fine,' Bill said. 'Can't wait for the weather to cheer up so I can get out in the garden again.'

'The first primroses are out and the snowdrops,' I said. 'It won't be long now.'

We chatted for a while and, as I got up to go, Betty said, 'Can I give a message to Jim for you? Save you phoning.'

'Oh, would you? It's just that Anthea wondered if he could pop into Brunswick Lodge sometime and see to the electrics in the Committee room. I'm not sure what's the matter, perhaps he could ring her. I expect he's got her number, but anyway she's in the book.'

'Jim's very good with electrics,' Betty said. 'He fixed our Hoover, just like that. I was ever so grateful. Well, you know what it's like if you have to have a man in – the amount they charge, just for coming out!'

'He's been marvellous at Brunswick Lodge,' I said. 'I don't know what we'd do without him now.'

'Doesn't have a lot to say for himself,' Betty went on, 'not like *her!* Not but what she's a good soul, do anything for you.'

'You're really lucky to have such nice neighbours.'

As Betty followed me into the hall to see me out I said, 'So good to see Bill right back on form again. You must have been so worried.'

'Oh, I was. It was a dreadful time, you know when things were so bad. All that going out at night and then not sleeping. Luckily I had some sleeping tablets the doctor gave me ages ago when I had that bad go of neuralgia. I don't usually take them – I sleep like a log, takes a lot to wake me! Anyway, they put him out like a light when he *did* go to bed.'

'They can be a blessing,' I said. 'I know Mother used to be very grateful for them sometimes when her arthritis was really bad. I must go. I've got to take some stuff for the jumble sale back to Brunswick Lodge.'

The rain had stopped but the air was still damp and there was a bitingly cold wind so I was really glad to get back home in the warm again. The animals made a quick dash out into the garden but were soon back in again, having in that short space of time managed to get their paws thoroughly wet and muddy. I contrived to catch Tris and wipe him clean, but I heard, to my dismay, Foss racing upstairs where he would, no doubt, be leaving muddy paw marks on my newly cleaned bedspread.

Since I was already awash with tea I decided that, since it had been quite a day, I deserved a gin and tonic. I was just trying to wrest the ice-cube tray from the freezer compartment that I should have defrosted days ago, when the phone rang. It was Brian.

'Sorry to bother you, Mrs Malory, but I thought you'd like to know that I went to see the police, like you said.'

'Oh, I'm so glad. How was it?'

'They were a bit awkward about it at first,

said I should have told them right away, but when I explained about Mother the Inspector was OK. He said he understood and was glad I'd come forward about it now. He was really nice. I was very relieved.'

'I expect he was glad to have it cleared up.'

'Yes, that's what he said.'

'Thank you so much for letting me know. I'm sure you feel better about it now.'

'Oh, and there was another thing. I've just had a phone call from David. He says he wants to come and talk to me about some way he might be able to help Mother. Like I said, he's been really nice.'

As I finally settled down with my drink I thought how incredible it was that so much good should have come from one man's death and how many lives had changed for the better because of it.

19

I got the review done eventually and was standing in the queue waiting to send it off at the post office when a voice behind me said,

'Why do they always have fewer people on the counter on pensions' days?'

It was Bridget.

'I know,' I said, 'and even those that are on duty go off for their elevenses when the queue stretches right outside the door!'

'Talking of elevenses,' Bridget said, 'do you feel like coming for a coffee when we get through this lot?'

'That would be nice.'

'There's a new place just opened, have you seen it? It's all lattes and bruschettas and tapenades. I must say I rather want to try it!'

'Taviscombe's answer to Starbucks!' I said when we were settled with our coffees (one cappuccino, one skinny latte). 'It's not very full, but I suppose in the Season it'll be better. Anyway, it makes a nice change from the dear old Buttery.'

'I rather wanted to have a word with you,' Bridget said, and I couldn't help contrasting this bright, lively Bridget with the mouse-like one I was used to.

'Oh yes?'

'David said he'd told you all about – you know – his father and everything.'

'Yes, I was glad he did. Of course I'd already learnt a lot about Sidney and how appalling he was from Brian.'

'Poor man! I haven't met him yet but from what David said he sounds a really good person. Actually,' she leaned forward and spoke confidentially, 'it's done David so much good to have someone to talk to about it, someone that's in the same boat, if you see what I mean.'

'I know Brian feels the same, and I gather that David thinks he might be able to do something about Brian's mother.'

'Yes, he's very anxious to do something there. Well, after the way he felt about his own mother and all she went through. He feels guilty, you know, though I've told him that's absolutely ridiculous and not to be an idiot.'

Certainly the old Bridget would never have thought of talking to David like that.

'What does he think can be done?'

'He's got a friend who's the head of the Psychiatry Department at one of the London teaching hospitals and he's going to ask him to help. Of course Mrs Thorpe may not agree, but she seems to trust David, so perhaps it might work out. Anyway, it's worth a try.'

'I think that's marvellous,' I said. 'If she could just be made well enough to accept Brian's Margaret and the children!'

'It would be marvellous, wouldn't it?'

'You know,' I said, 'I was thinking just the other day how much good had come out of that terrible man's death.'

'It's amazing, isn't it? David's certainly a different person. I can hardly believe it sometimes.'

'And you're different too.'

'Well, he didn't affect me like he did David, of course. David kept me away as much as he could, and the boys too. Goodness, it *is* wonderful to have them home. But before I never knew where I was with David. His moods changed from one minute to the other. Honestly, Sheila, there were times when I was quite frightened.'

'It must have been really upsetting for you both.'

'It's wonderful now, we can be a proper

normal family at last. And, do you know, David hasn't had one of his migraines for weeks.'

'Oh, poor soul, migraines are awful. I used to have them myself, but mercifully I seem to have grown out of them in my old age. I suppose David's were caused by stress?'

'I think so. He used to have them quite a lot. Actually he had one on the night his father died.'

'Did he?'

'Yes, a really bad one. Well, you'd know what it's like. He had to go to bed straight after supper and the medication didn't work so he had a wretched night.'

'All night?' I asked sharply.

She looked at me curiously. 'Yes. And part of the next day, too.'

'But that gives him an alibi for when his father was killed. Didn't you tell the police?'

'When they asked he said he was at home all evening and I confirmed that – he said he wasn't very well.'

'But surely everyone knows that if you have a bad migraine, it's absolutely crippling. You can hardly move, let alone *do* anything.'

'Perhaps only people who've actually had one... Anyway, there's no way of proving it, is there? We might have been just saying that, why should they believe us?'

I kept thinking of David's migraine all day and wondering what I should do. It might all be an invention to give him an alibi. He may have hoped that I'd believe the story and pass it on to Roger, who he knew was a friend of mine. After all, although I knew Bridget quite well, she didn't usually invite me to have coffee with her, so why had she done so today? Perhaps I just wanted to believe her and had seized upon anything that would clear David of the murder. And yet there had been something about the way she told me that rang true. I couldn't believe that Bridget – even the new Bridget – would be able to lie so convincingly.

I told Rosemary about it next day

'Oh, migraines are *awful*,' she said. 'Colin used to have them, do you remember? We used to be desperately worried in case he got one on the day of an exam, but he never did. He used to say that you only ever get them when you're *able* to have them, like weekends or holidays.'

'I think he's right,' I said, 'now I come to think of it. Though I don't know how that helps us decide whether or not David really did have one the night Sidney was killed.'

'I don't know if Colin still has them or

not,' Rosemary said thoughtfully. 'That's the worst of him being so far away in Canada. It's not the sort of thing he'd ever think of telling me and if I asked him he'd probably say no, he didn't, so's not to worry me.'

'I know,' I agreed. 'When Michael was at Oxford he came off his motor bike and injured his leg quite badly, but he never said a word and I only heard about it ages after when one of his friends mentioned it. But then boys never tell you anything. Even now, if I want to know anything I have to ask Thea!'

'Delia's just at the age when she never stops talking,' Rosemary said. 'Mind you, I sometimes haven't the faintest idea of what she's talking *about*. I think all grandparents should be given a crash course in pop and fashion. Just you wait till Alice is that age. Though I suppose it'll be all different then, things seem to move so fast nowadays.'

'I know. When we were young things moved slowly, gradually – until the sixties, I suppose, then it all speeded up. Anyway,' I said, 'what am I going to do about telling Roger? Do you think I should?'

'I don't see how it would do any harm,' Rosemary said. 'In any case he may have drawn his own conclusions, he's no fool.'

'No, of course not. I have the greatest respect for Roger's intelligence, but if he hasn't got all the facts...?'

'True.'

'Well, he knows about Brian's alibi by now,' I said, 'so David's more or less his last remaining suspect.'

'Oh, *bother* Sidney Middleton,' Rosemary said fiercely. 'He's still causing trouble and messing up people's lives even after he's dead. I'm going to put the kettle on. Tea or coffee?'

I was still wondering what to do the following morning when I met Roger quite by chance.

I was just taking my car in for a service when I met Roger coming out.

'Hello. Trouble with the car?'

'Oh, hello, Roger. No, just a service. How about you?'

'A couple of new tyres. How are you getting back, would you like a lift home?'

'Well, I was going to walk, but it's such a miserable day, so yes, please. Can you hang on while I just hand the keys in?'

Sitting beside Roger in the car it seemed silly not to tell him about David.

'That's what Bridget told me,' I concluded,

'and I think it's the truth.'

'Could be,' Roger said.

'I mean, if he was going to come up with an invented migraine story,' I said, 'why wouldn't he have told you about it straight away? Why wait till now?'

'True.' Roger stopped and waved a vacillating pensioner on over the pedestrian crossing.

'He's the person with the strongest motive, so I can't rule him out, but I'm inclined to agree with you. Which leaves me with absolutely no one in the frame. Your tip about Joseph came to nothing.'

'Yes, I'm sorry about that. I was going to ring you when Michael filled me in about him. You must blame your grandmother-in-law for not coming up to scratch on that one!'

'Extraordinary! First time I've ever known it to happen.'

'Well, you must remember she was ill in bed at the time and not up to her usual high standard of information gathering.'

Roger laughed. 'I'd hate to think one of my primary sources was failing.'

'So what happens now?' I asked.

'I'm following the only other line left,' he said. 'I'm making enquiries at the London end. I've been getting all sorts of whispers and half-hints of some sort of shady dealing.'

'Jack said that there'd been rumours. But, as I'm sure I said before, anyone from London would be really quite noticeable in Taviscombe if they'd come down to do the deed.'

'It doesn't necessarily have to be someone from London,' Roger said. 'After all, Sidney Middleton did give financial advice and it's quite possible he gave the wrong sort of advice to someone down here. You know, really bad advice that might have ruined them.'

'Of course! That's quite possible. So it could be anyone.'

'I'll go on making enquiries, but it's going to be a long job. People aren't too keen to talk about such things.'

'No, I suppose not.'

'Right then, here you are.'

'Thank you so much. Will you come in for a cup of something?'

'I'd love to, but duty calls.'

I went about my household tasks that day with a lighter heart. It was a great relief to know that Roger didn't believe David was the murderer. Totally illogical, of course, but

I suppose we would none of us like to think that one of our acquaintance is a killer, however great the provocation may have been.

As I was dusting the living room I came to the small Victorian table Sidney had left me in his will. I stood for a while looking at it, then, with a sudden resolution I picked it up and took it out to the garage.

'It's no good,' I said to Foss who had followed me out in search of the possibility of entertainment, 'I can't stand it in the house any longer. It reminds me of how that man fooled us all. I think I'll give it to the jumble sale.'

Foss, however, was busy hunting down spiders in the cobwebby corner of the garage and took no notice.

Brian came the next day to finish painting the bookcases and I told him about David's migraine.

'I think Inspector Eliot believes him,' I said, 'so it looks as if David has an alibi too.'

'That's wonderful. I was really worried about him. He's been so good to us. Did you hear about what he's trying to do for Mother?'

'Yes, Bridget told me. Do you think she'll agree to see anyone?'

'I don't know. We'll have to go really slowly, but she trusts him, more than she trusts me in some ways, but that's fine by me if it means she'll have the treatment.'

'Have you told Margaret?'

'Yes. We're just holding our breath.'

'I do hope it all works out for you.'

While Brian was working on the bookcases I busied myself in the kitchen making some cakes for the refreshment stall at the jumble sale. I always find it soothing to measure and mix and bake, a pleasant, almost mindless occupation, especially with the radio on in the background. This time it was a money programme with various experts talking about investments, equities and the financial world in general. It was not exactly easy listening, but the occasional sentence filtered through into my mind and I found myself wondering about Sidney's dealings in the City, and possibly, as Roger had said, down here. We'd known that when he'd first retired and come back to Taviscombe to live, he'd acted as a financial adviser (though I don't think it was called that then) to various people. I tried to think if I'd known who any of them had been. I had a vague memory of my mother's old friend Mrs Warburton talking about how he'd helped her, and *her* friend Miss Chapman. Sidney was always very good with old ladies. But they were both dead long since and neither of them had any close relatives who might have had any reason to hold a grudge against Sidney over his financial dealings. Miss Chapman, I recalled, had caused a great deal of talk by leaving most of her money to the curate at St James, for whom she had cherished a respectable regard for many years. But there must have been others and no doubt Roger would find them. It was some sort of motive, after all.

As I was thinking about all this Brian came into the kitchen.

'I've finished the bookcases,' he began. 'Oh, I'm sorry, were you listening to that?'

'Listening? Oh, the radio. I'd forgotten it was on.'

'Those money programmes,' Brian said. 'They can be quite interesting. There was one very good one I heard about insurance.'

'Yes, they're quite useful.' I moved over and switched the radio off. 'Shall we have a cup of tea? I know I can do with one after all this baking.'

'That would be very nice.'

'I don't know much about finance and

things,' Brian said. 'Though I used to hear *him* talking about it sometimes.'

'Really?'

'Well, not so much talking – he knew my mother hadn't a clue about anything like that – but boasting.'

'What about?'

'Oh, deals he'd made, how he'd put something over on someone.'

'In the City?'

'That's right. He was just sounding off about things, he knew she hadn't any idea what he was talking about. Just wanted someone to know how clever he was.'

'He didn't say what sort of deals, did he?'

'He may have done, but it didn't mean anything to me either, I was just a kid.'

'No, of course.'

'That's just the way he was in those days, though I don't suppose he changed much, except to make even dodgier deals and get richer.'

'You think the deals he made in those days were dodgy?'

'Oh yes, no doubt about it. It was the way he talked about them, even though I didn't understand I could tell there was something not right about them. It was all of a piece with the rest of him, I reckon.'

'I'm sure you're right.'

When we'd finished our tea I went to have a look at the shelves.

'They're lovely,' I said. 'They improve the look of the whole room.'

'Well,' Brian said, regarding the piles of books on the floor, 'it's somewhere to put all that lot. Mind you, that paint will take a fair while to dry properly, so don't put any books on the shelves for at least a fortnight.'

When he had gone I went back into the kitchen and checked on the cakes in the oven. One was done so I put it on the wire tray to cool and re-set the timer for the other. There was still some tea left in the pot so I poured myself another cup and sat down at the kitchen table to think about what Brian had told me. I had no doubt now that the young Sidney Middleton had been less than scrupulous in his financial dealings and, as Brian had said, there was no reason to suppose that he had become more honest with the passing years. He'd certainly become richer and I hoped that Roger would be able to find out just how he'd managed it, and if that was why he'd been killed.

20

'What's that little table doing there?' Anthea asked.

'I brought it to go in the sale,' I said.

Anthea bent down to examine it. 'It's an antique,' she said. 'Are you sure you want to get rid of it?'

'Yes. Quite sure.'

'Oh, all right then. Put it over there with the bric-a-brac. Now then, about the clothes.' She looked round. 'I thought Rosemary was coming too.'

'Yes, she is, she'll be here in a little while.'

'Well, you'll have to tell her about where things are to go. I can't stop to go all over it again when she comes.'

'That's all right.'

Anthea looked at the garments piled up on one of the trestle tables. 'We don't get nearly as many things as we used to,' she said. 'It's all those charity shops.'

'I suppose it's more convenient to get rid of things as and when,' I said, 'instead of keeping them hanging around until the next jumble sale.'

'That's as may be,' Anthea said irritably, 'but if this goes on we'll have to give up the clothing stall altogether. You'll just have to make this lot look as attractive as you can.'

'I daresay if we price things cheaply enough they'll go anyway.'

Anthea gave me a dissatisfied look and went on, 'Put the coats and dresses on the rail and fold the other stuff neatly and lay it out on the table. The hats and shoes should go separately at one end.'

'That's fine,' I said, 'I'm sure we can manage.'

'Right then, I must be going. Oh, by the way, Jim Norton is in the Committee Room seeing to the electrics. I expect he would like a cup of tea when you and Rosemary make one.'

When she had gone I trundled out the rail on wheels that we used on these occasions from the store room and was just trying to disentangle some of the pile of metal coat-hangers that seemed irretrievably entwined when Rosemary arrived.

'Sorry I'm late, Jack suddenly decided to come home for lunch so I had to cook something. Has Anthea gone?'

'Your absence was noted,' I said, 'and I

have strict instructions to pass on all the vital information she gave me about the disposition of the merchandise. All the same as last year, of course. Here, you can unlock these hangers and I'll put the things on the rail.'

'Anything decent this time?' Rosemary asked, turning over the garments on the table. 'Oh, this is pretty.' She held up a girl's pink top with rosebuds round the neckline. 'A year ago I'd have got it for Delia, but I wouldn't *dare* choose anything for her now. She was very polite about the top I gave her for her birthday but I could see that she didn't think it was really *cool*.'

'I did have my eye on that little straw hat for Alice, that one over there with the cornflowers and poppies on it. If I price it quite high then I won't feel guilty at having first pick!'

'The children's things are always the first to go,' Rosemary said, 'and some of the sweaters. This one's pure wool and, good-ness, this one's cashmere!'

'Oh, that'll be Marjorie Richards, she always sends expensive stuff. *I* think it's a form of showing off, but who cares if it sells well!'

'Is this leather coat hers as well?'

'No, I recognise that, it's Beryl Austin's – she used to wear it when she went around with Jimmy Hackett in that open-top sports car of his. When they broke up I suppose she didn't want it any more.'

'I didn't know that they'd broken up,' Rosemary said with interest. *That* didn't last long – young people nowadays!'

'This rail is very wobbly,' I said. 'It's not straight, the things keep sliding to one end.'

I bent down to examine it more closely. 'Oh yes, this nut needs tightening. Have we got a spanner or something?' I fiddled with it for a moment, then I said, 'I'll go and ask Jim Norton if he's got one. He's in the Committee room. Oh yes, and Anthea said very pointedly that *when* – not if – we make our cup of tea would we give him one.'

'Right, then,' Rosemary said, 'I'll go and put the kettle on.'

I found Jim Norton crouching on the floor rewiring a point.

'Do you have a spanner I could borrow, please? The rail we hang the clothes on needs fixing.'

'Can you manage?' he asked. 'I'd come and do it for you now but I'm in the middle of something.'

'No, it's fine, just a simple job. I can do it.'

'Right. There's a couple of spanners in my big tool box. I left it in the big room over by the window, help yourself.'

I thanked him and found it where he had told me. It was a big, blue metal box with a folding lid and with two layers for tools and odds and ends. I found a spanner in the size I wanted but I couldn't close the box up again. Something underneath was preventing the top layer from lying flat, so I lifted up the tray to repack it. As I did so there was a familiar acrid smell and I found in the bottom of the toolbox a pair of rough leather gardening gloves, covered in soot. Not only were they stained black, but grains of soot were caught in the leather fibres.

I took them out of the box and stood there considering what I had found. There was a stifled exclamation behind me and I turned to see Jim Norton staring at the gloves in my hand.

For a moment neither of us said anything. Then I said, 'Soot,' holding out the gloves.

'Yes,' he said. 'I was – I was clearing out the grate...'

'No,' I said. 'That's not it. I saw your face, you were horrified when you saw what I'd found.' He was silent and I continued, 'Besides, you don't have a grate. You don't have a chimney. The soot on those gloves came from Sidney Middleton's inspection plate, didn't it? I daresay it could be proved...' My voice trailed away.

He still didn't say anything but just stood there, motionless.

'But why? What possible reason could *you* have for killing him?'

'I've put the kettle on, tea won't be long.' Rosemary came back into the room. She looked from one to another of us. 'What's going on?'

'Why?' I persisted. 'Why did you kill Sidney Middleton? You did kill him, didn't you?'

Rosemary's exclamation of surprise seemed to bring Jim Norton back to life.

'Yes,' he said in a steady tone. 'I did it. I had my reasons.'

'But why?'

'He killed my son.'

'Your son? How, what happened?'

'So I killed him.'

'No!' The word was positively shouted. Myra Norton had come into the room. She moved towards us and saw the gloves I was still holding in my hands. 'No, he didn't do it, he didn't do it!'

Jim Norton moved over and grasped her

294

arm. 'Be quiet, Myra. It's all right. I'll deal with this.'

She broke free and confronted us.

'It was me. I did it and I'm not ashamed to admit it. He – that man – he killed Martin, he killed my son, the only one we had left. Julie, my girl, she died of meningitis, so Martin was all we had, and he took him away from us...' She was sobbing now. Jim Norton put his arm round her awkwardly, as if it was a rare gesture for him.

'Martin worked in the City,' he said. 'He lived with us – he could have got a place of his own, but he knew how much it meant to his mother to have him at home. So he travelled up from Reading every day.He was a bright boy and did very well, they all thought highly of him. Middleton was impressed and made him his assistant. But Middleton was up to all sorts of scams. Martin never knew about them, of course, he was too straight himself to think of any-one doing things like that. A fool, perhaps, but honest, honest as the day is long. Anyway, the long and the short of it was Middleton tried to pull off some really big thing – something to do with insider trading, I won't go into details – and it went wrong. But Middleton was really clever. He'd got it all worked out that if it did go wrong then Martin would get the blame for it.'

'They took him away,' Myra Norton sobbed. 'They came to the house and took him away.'

'There was a court case,' Jim Norton said quietly, 'and Martin was convicted and sent to jail. They put him in an ordinary jail at first. They were going to move him to an open prison – that's what they usually do for fraud cases – but those couple of weeks were too much for him. He couldn't bear it and he hanged himself.'

'Oh God!' Rosemary said quietly.

'Myra here had a breakdown,' Jim Norton said. 'She's still on anti-depressants, will be for the rest of her life.'

'Did you know that Sidney Middleton lived in Taviscombe when you moved down here?' I asked.

'No. We came here because it's where we used to bring the children on holiday when they were small. It had happy memories for us.'

'They used to play on the sands,' Myra Norton said, tears pouring down her face. 'They had ice creams...'

'I'm sorry,' I said inadequately. 'I'm so sorry.'

She moved suddenly towards me and, instinctively, I backed away.

'You've got a son,' she cried, 'and you,' turning to Rosemary, 'you'd have done the same.'

I found I still had the gloves and I held them out to Jim Norton.

'Why didn't you get rid of them?' I asked.

'I thought Myra had,' he said, taking them from me. 'I don't know why she didn't.'

'To remind us,' she said fiercely, 'so we'd never forget!'

Jim Norton moved over to her side. 'When I saw that man here – at that auction, it was – I couldn't believe it. I knew what it would do to Myra, so I decided I'd have to get rid of him. I went round to his house when I knew he was going to be away (I heard you talking about it here) and as soon as I saw the inspection plate I knew how to do it. Neighbours of ours in Reading nearly died from carbon monoxide poisoning when theirs was left off by mistake. We went round one night. Myra insisted on coming with me...'

'But he couldn't do it!' she burst out. 'When it came to it he couldn't do it. So I did. I did. He killed Martin. An eye for an eye...'

'We went back just before it got light,' he went on, 'and put the plate back. I had a torch but it was dark and I must have missed seeing the soot that fell out. I thought the Goddards might have heard the car so early in the morning, but they didn't.'

'He didn't do it,' Myra Norton was shouting now, shouting wildly and sobbing at the same time. 'I did it, I did it!'

Her husband moved over and put his arm round her shoulder.

'It's all right,' he said, 'we're going home, we're going home.'

He led her away and, just as they got to the door he turned and said, 'You don't have to worry, we'll do the right thing.' Then they were gone.

I sank down into a chair. 'That woman, that poor woman.'

'Dreadful,' Rosemary said. 'Dreadful,' she repeated.

'What have I done?' I said. 'Oh why did I have to interfere?'

'She was living on the edge,' Rosemary said. 'I see that now – all that endless chatter.'

'But I pushed her over the edge. I should never have done that.'

'She shouldn't have killed Sidney. I know,

an eye for an eye, but where does that end? It's terrible, I know, but you have to accept it. It wasn't your fault.'

'But would we have done the same if it had happened to our children?'

'No,' Rosemary said, 'we would have wanted to, but we wouldn't have done it.'

'He took the gloves,' I said suddenly. 'We have no proof. There's nothing to tell the police. I'm glad about that.'

'I think he will go to the police himself,' Rosemary said. 'I think he probably wanted to all along.'

'But Myra – what will happen to her?'

'Diminished responsibility, I imagine. She's obviously unbalanced.'

'I just wish I'd never interfered...'

Rosemary came and put her arm round me.

'There's no point in blaming yourself,' she said. 'It's something that was always going to end in unhappiness. It's not your fault. Come back now and have some supper with Jack and me.'

I looked at the piles of clothing. 'What about all this?' I asked.

'We'll do it tomorrow. Tomorrow's another day.'

'Yes,' I said. 'I suppose it is.'

The publishers hope that this book has given you enjoyable reading. Large Print Books are especially designed to be as easy to see and hold as possible. If you wish a complete list of our books please ask at your local library or write directly to:

Magna Large Print Books
Magna House, Long Preston,
Skipton, North Yorkshire.
BD23 4ND

This Large Print Book, for people
who cannot read normal print,
is published under the auspices of

THE ULVERSCROFT FOUNDATION

This Large Print Book for people who cannot read normal print, is published under the auspices of

THE ULVERSCROFT FOUNDATION

..., we hope you have enjoyed this book. Please think for a moment about those who have worse sight than you and are unable to read, enjoy a book, magazine or newspaper.

You can help them by sending a donation, large or small, to:

**The Ulverscroft Foundation,
The Green, Bradgate Road,
Anstey, Leicestershire LE7 7FU,
England**

or request a copy of our brochure for more details.

The Foundation will use all donations to assist those people who are severely handicapped and need special attention with medical research, diagnosis and treatment.

Thank you very much for your help.